The Curious Adventures
of Jimmy McGee

The Curious Adventures of Jimmy McGee

Eleanor Estes

With illustrations by John O'Brien

AN ODYSSEY/HARCOURT YOUNG CLASSIC

HARCOURT, INC.

Orlando   Austin   New York   San Diego   Toronto   London

To Polly

Text copyright © 1987 by Eleanor Estes
Illustrations copyright © 1987 by John O'Brien

www.HarcourtBooks.com

First Harcourt Young Classics edition 2005
First Odyssey Classics edition 2005
First published 1987

Library of Congress Cataloging-in-Publication Data
Estes, Eleanor, 1906–1988.
The curious adventures of Jimmy McGee/Eleanor Estes;
illustrated by John O'Brien.
p.   cm.
Summary: A tiny plumber becomes a hero by
rescuing a doll and returning it to its grateful owner.
[1. Heroes—Fiction.   2. Dolls—Fiction.   3. Fantasy.]
I. O'Brien, John, 1953– ill.   II. Title.
PZ7.E749Cu   2005
[Fic]—dc22   2005040247
ISBN-13: 978-0152-05523-3   ISBN-10: 0-15-205523-1
ISBN-13: 978-0152-05517-2 (pb)   ISBN-10: 0-15-205517-7 (pb)

Text set in Bodoni Classico
Designed by Kaelin Chappell

Printed in the United States of America

A C E G H F D B
A C E G H F D B (pb)

Who Is Jimmy McGee?

Do you think he's a gnome?
Well, that he might be
If we ransacked the scrolls
In his pipe library.
And if we did find them,
Could we unravel the script
And trace the odd tale of his own family tree?
But this much we know. A plumber is he,
This grand little man named Jimmy McGee.

CONTENTS

The Curious Adventures
of Jimmy McGee

1

Amy's *Who's Who Book*

At first Jimmy McGee didn't know he was a hero. He never even thought what he was. Just a busy fellow, a plumber, mainly. Banging on pipes, waking people up, fixing things, making faucets stop dripping, going here, going there...zoomie-zoomie. That was his business.

But one day he found himself on a page in a book. The name of this book was the *Who's Who Book* by Amy. It was a little brown-red notebook that happened to open, as if by magic, to the M page. He read this:

McGee, Jimmy: a little fellow, a plumber, a banger on pipes, a HERO.

That's what astonished him...HERO! Why hero? The rest of what the book said about him was correct. But why, why hero? He had to try to find an answer to this startling question.

It was an evening during the summer, and the place was a little cottage in Truro on Cape Cod. The cottage, named The Bizzy Bee, was high up on a dune at the beach. The little girl Amy, who wrote that book, her mother, her father, who was a teacher and had all summer for a vacation, and their great dog, a dark brown-and-white springer spaniel named Wags, were the people who called this cottage their summer headquarters. Spending the summer with Amy was her best friend, Clarissa. Both Amy and Clarissa had long blond hair and blue eyes; both were seven, going on eight, and in the same class in school.

Amy didn't know where Jimmy McGee's summer headquarters were. Nobody knew. Most people didn't even know about Jimmy McGee at all. But Amy did. Otherwise she would not have put him in her *Who's Who Book* in the M's.

The family had only just arrived in the old gray Dodge and were bringing in their luggage and cartons, putting them in the right rooms of The Bizzy Bee. While the big people were unloading, Amy and Clarissa raced around the

cottage. At the front, which faced the sea, they stood, silent, at the top of the dune and looked out at the wide, wide ocean. They flung back their arms, took in deep breaths of the pure ocean air, and watched the waves come rolling in and break on the sunny, sandy beach way down below.

Amy said, "Clarissa. It's a rule that we cannot roll down, down the dune to the sandy beach. You'd like to, I know. So would I. But it's a rule my mama and papa made, and they don't make many. When they do, they always have a good reason. Here, Clarissa, you know the sand of the dune might collapse and come pouring down on you and smother you to smithereens."

"O-o-oh!" Clarissa gasped. She drew back from the wispy weeds at the top of the edge of the dune.

Amy laughed. "Well," she said. "Now, we'll go over there. There are steps there. Twenty-six in all. Just like the alphabet."

These steps led down to the beach and were only about fifteen feet from the front of The Bizzy Bee.

At the top of the gray weather-beaten wooden stairs there was a little platform with a bench to sit on. There Amy and Clarissa and Amy's mother and father and their friends could sit and shake the sand off their wet towels, wipe off their feet, relax, and watch the seagulls, screaming and swooping down to fight over something they thought was good to eat.

Clarissa watched them in fascination. This was the time of day, late in the afternoon, when they were likely to find their best pickings. They'd make a dive for something. Even if it was nothing to eat, they all thought it might be.

Now, Amy and Clarissa watched the last few straggling people, who had stayed the longest, gather up their things to go home to dinner. Tiredly they plodded down the beach a ways to their own stairs. Each cottage had about twenty-six steps from the beach to the dune above.

"Tomorrow we'll be doing that," said Amy happily. "Too late this afternoon."

Amy fumbled around in the pocket of her blue sweater. "Ah!" she said. "Here it is! Got stuck in a loose stitch." She took out her special red-brown notebook that she almost always carried around with her in case she needed to write something in it. She showed it to Clarissa.

The *Who's Who Book* by Amy was the name of it. It was a little frayed and bent at the edges, but Clarissa saw at once that it was a very important book. "A book of names," said Amy happily.

Clarissa held the book for a moment carefully as though she were holding a rare treasure. Then the book opened itself to the M page. Amy said, "It's a sort of magic book. It always opens itself to the M page. That's the L page, too, right ahead of the M's. Even after you think you have closed the book tightly, it always springs back to the L and M page. I should put an elastic band around it, but I won't."

"Why do you 'spose it does that?" Clarissa asked curiously.

"Because it's the magic page that has the name of Jimmy McGee on it," said Amy. "He's..."

Without waiting to hear more, Clarissa interrupted. "Am I in it, that book of names of yours?"

"Of course," said Amy. "Book begins with 'A for Amy, a little girl, age 7.'

"'B for Bear...my Teddy Bear, age 3.' Now C for...guess who?"

"Me!" exclaimed Clarissa, delighted.

"Yes," said Amy. She put her finger on the C's.... "C for 'Clarissa, a little girl, age 7. Amy's friend.'"

Clarissa smiled. "How can you be in a book and out of a book at the same time?" she asked.

"Can," said Amy. "Same as being in and out of a mirror at the same time."

"Oh, of course!" said Clarissa.

"Begins with Amy, that's me. Ends with Z," said Amy.

"Z! What doll or person do you have under Z?" asked Clarissa.

"'Z: Zazoom, a clown doll,'" said Amy. "Zoomie-zoomies are named after him."

Clarissa laughed. "'Zoomie-zoomies!'" she said. "What's that?"

"O-o-oh," said Amy. "It's a magic that can make people who have it do curious things," she said. "Maybe even animals, maybe even a doll. Well, it's magic."

"Did you bring Zazoom with you?" asked Clarissa.

"No," said Amy. "Couldn't bring all the dolls and clowns and everybody. I brought Little Lydia, named after Lydia, Big...you know, the doll who swallowed the thermometer. Left her home...too big. The only doll I brought is Little Lydia, and see? She is on the line right above 'McGee, Jimmy.' See?"

"Is my doll—I did bring her—Pee-Wee, in it?" asked Clarissa.

"Yes," said Amy. "And Wags is in it, and all my family..."

Amy closed the book. But it sprang open again to the M page. "See?" she said. "It always does that. There he is! 'McGee, Jimmy: a little fellow, a plumber, a banger on pipes, a HERO.'"

Clarissa said, "Why do you call Jimmy McGee a hero?"

"Because," said Amy, "he always has to do such hard things, such very hard things, hard and curious, that no one else has ever even thought to try to do."

"Oh my, yes, of course!" said Clarissa. "He is a hero all right."

Clarissa asked if she could hold this important book for a minute and see if it flipped back to the M's if *she* were holding it. "I'll be careful," she said.

Amy handed Clarissa the book. Holding the book tightly in her little fist, she recited as though it were a lesson in school, "A is for Amy, B is for Bear, C is for me, Clarissa…" She paused. "That's all I'll say now. It's enough to make the test." She then placed the book in her lap. Right away it sprang open to the M page. "Well! What do you know? Your book is magic, too."

Amy laughed. "Likes the letter M and the letter L," she said.

Amy and Clarissa laughed and laughed and did the "Open Book!" test over and over. It never failed. "Likes McGee, Jimmy. Likes Lydia, Little!"

"All the same," said Clarissa, "I want to know more. Jimmy McGee must be more than a name in your *Who's Who Book,* Amy. Exactly *who* is Jimmy McGee? Where does he live, for instance?"

At that moment there came a great whambang on the pipes in the cellar of The Bizzy Bee.

"Hear that?" asked Amy. She laughed gleefully. "*That's* Jimmy McGee! He's just turned on the water, so we'll have water to drink and to cook with and everything. He'll do all kinds of things to open up this house. Papa will say, 'Well, I'll be ding-busted! Know this cottage so well, I do things even in my sleep!'"

"So!" said Clarissa. "What I hear is Jimmy McGee, wham-banger of pipes, turner-on of water...?"

"Uh-huh!" said Amy.

"Listen, Amy," said Clarissa. "Why don't we race over to the cottage and try to look through the cellar window? If that little fellow named Jimmy McGee is down there, wham-banging like all get-out, well, maybe we'd see him. I'm in the book and out of the book...maybe same thing about him!"

"Oh," said Amy. "By now he's not in the cellar. Listen!"

There came another wham-bang. "Now he's turned the water on in the kitchen, and now, as fast as that, he's turned on the outside faucet. He's letting them all run to get the rusty water out," said Amy.

"Well," said Clarissa with a sigh, "at least now I know *who* Jimmy McGee is, banger on pipes as you have it in your book. And hearing is almost as good as seeing."

"Believing is best of all," said Amy.

Another bang shuddered the cottage. "Goodness knows what pipe he is banging now!" Amy's eyes were shining with excitement.

"Tub, shower...bathroom things," suggested Clarissa. "I like this game!"

"This is not a game," said Amy sternly. "You don't call Jimmy McGee and his way of fixing things in a jiffy a game! Gosh, Clarissa!"

"He's a great man." Clarissa corrected herself hastily. "A hero! So it is written in your great book on page 13, your *Who's Who Book*. Wish I knew how to write books."

"You could try. Got all summer," said Amy. "But you're right. He's a little man, but great. Everybody doesn't know about him."

"Anyway, I wish I knew a little bit more than I do so far about Jimmy McGee. Besides being a banger on pipes."

"Oh," said Amy. "There's plenty to learn. Ever put your ear against a telephone pole? Hear the humming there? That's Jimmy McGee using his magic..."

"...his zoomie-zoomies," interrupted Clarissa.

"Yes," said Amy. "Going off on some curious adventure! As the summer goes on, we'll learn more about him."

Amy spoke absentmindedly. With her finger as if glued to the L and M page, she said, "You see that Little Lydia is right above McGee.

There might be a curious connection here, Clarissa. We have to ferret it out. Two heads are better than one."

Clarissa smiled and looked happily at her friend. But then there was another slam-bang so loud that Clarissa was ready to fly down the twenty-six steps.

Amy grabbed her skirt. "Don't worry," she said calmly. "He's just zoomed off to the cottage next door. It echoes. All the way up and down the beach he'll be going from cottage to cottage on Cape Cod, and then on and on, to Maine even! Maybe even to Lebanon, where that real Lydia, who gave me the two Lydia dolls, lives. Maybe he'll even zoomie-zoomie over to some of the little islands in the ocean."

Clarissa liked that. She sat down again. "Zoomie-zoomie!"

They both began to laugh so hard that tears ran down their cheeks.

But Clarissa was persistent. "Amy," she said. "What *do* you think he looks like? Can't see him...just hear him piping here, piping there. Well, what *do* you think he looks like?"

"Sh-sh-sh," said Amy. "I'm thinking about it...what he might look like."

Amy placed her little book, open to the M page, beside her on the bench. She cupped her chin in her hands, looked out over the ocean, and thought about the little plumber, the banger on pipes...Jimmy McGee.

Dreamily, Amy and Clarissa watched the big red sun being sucked down into the sea. Suddenly it went down altogether. Then such a lovely afterglow spread over the sky and the ocean that sky and ocean seemed to become one.

Amy's mother came out of the cottage. "My!" she said. "How beautiful! But come in now," she said. "The water's on, everything is fixed, and dinner's ready. Fish!"

"Fish!" exclaimed Amy. "Many bones in it?"

"Not too many," said Mama. "Imagine! Fresh mackerel, caught just this morning. I'll help with the bones."

As they walked to the cottage, Clarissa said, "In bed tonight please try to explain to me what you think Jimmy McGee looks like, what he wears, for instance, where he sleeps, eats, everything?"

Amy said, "Oh, yes. I thought about it while the sun was sinking. I'll tell you in bed tonight."

But when they went in, Amy forgot to tuck

her little *Who's Who Book* back in her pocket. There it lay on the gray wooden bench. A light breeze fluttered the pages, but always fluttered them back to the M page.

In bed that night, Clarissa asked sleepily, "Who...where is Jimmy McGee? I might dream about him."

"I might, too," said Amy. "But I'm too tired now. I'm going to zoomie-zoomie to...sleep."

"Me, too," said Clarissa. "I love that word... zoo-ooom..." And she fell asleep.

So did Amy.

They both went sound asleep. But Jimmy McGee did not. When he came back to his summer headquarters near the top of the dune in front of Amy's house, he saw Amy's *Who's Who Book* on the dew-moist bench. It was open as usual to the M page. What he saw was this:

McGee, Jimmy: a little fellow, a plumber, a banger on pipes, a HERO.

The rest of it was true. "But, hero?" he exclaimed. "Why hero?"

That's what puzzled him and why *he* didn't go to sleep.

2

Jimmy McGee in His Summer Headquarters

That night Jimmy McGee certainly had not gone right off to sleep as Amy and Clarissa had. It was all on account of that book, the *Who's Who Book* by Amy.

Until evening, the day had gone as usual for him. When he had finished his usual rounds, turning on faucets, fixing broken things, banging pipes all up and down the beach and way, way away, he had to go back to his headquarters for a special tool for a special job.

It was then that on the little wooden bench at the top of the dune he spotted the little red-brown notebook, flipped open to a page where he saw his name. Puzzled, he picked it up, read the name of it, and what it said about him. While mulling over why he was mentioned in such a curious way…hero…he thought he should pick the book up and put it in his tool bag. Otherwise, it might blow away in the night, and Amy would never see it again. And neither would he! In the morning early, he would put it back, and Amy would never even know it had been on an adventure because it would be all nice and sunny and dry.

So he did that special hard job he had to do down Pawtucket way and came back to his headquarters. He really was very curious to see what else besides himself was in this book. He stretched out on a little hammock he had slung up in his headquarters, between two sturdy roots.

Jimmy McGee's summer headquarters were very near that platform at the top of the twenty-six steps where he had found this odd book. They were in a little cave under the hard, grassy ledge that ran along the top of the dune all up and down the beach. Sitting up there on the wooden platform, neither Amy nor anybody else would know that there was this snug little cave nearby, nor that Jimmy McGee, the little banger on pipes, had his summer headquarters in it. And no one could see in. Straggling roots of

tough sea grass made a tattered, lacy curtain that concealed the entranceway. Anyway, no one would even think to look there.

His summer headquarters were small. But they were big enough for him and his things because he and his things were little, too. If any creature at all should wander in, he or she might acquire a touch of magic because Jimmy McGee himself was magic. But he had few visitors... now and then a wandering cricket or a curious beetle, but they would soon wander back out not knowing they had been touched by magic.

Jimmy McGee made himself comfortable in his hammock, and he chewed on a piece of beech plum root and prepared to read this book of Amy's. He wanted to see what a book like this that had him in it said. A leisurely rest of this sort was most unusual for Jimmy McGee. Generally he allowed himself only one-two secs from his rounds for a nap of one-two secs. This showed what a strong hold this little book had on him.

He opened it up with curious anticipation. Right away he saw that the book was written in alphabetical order. He knew the alphabet; in fact, he knew how to read, and in many languages. He tended the nuts and bolts and the pipes of the library in Washington, D.C., near his winter headquarters, which were in Mount Rose Park. If he read something that he liked, he would make a copy of it in his own bebop code and store it in his little pipe library.

To be really comfortable, he now took off his stovepipe hat and hung it on a handy grassy root to the left of his hammock. He had made this hat out of a small piece of black stovepipe that he'd found in the alleyway behind Amy's house in Washington, D.C. It must once have been part of a kind of parlor stove because it was so small, not big like a kitchen stovepipe would be. He had made a top for it out of a tin stove-flue covering, which he had had to cut down quite a little to make it fit. Although the middle of this flue covering had had a pretty picture of a waterfall, he had blackened it out because he wanted his whole hat to be black. He had bent up the bottom of the stovepipe hat neatly and rounded it so he could tip his hat if he wanted to. He kept the hat shined with stove polish from a nearly empty can he'd also found. His hat was really quite elegant . . . a sort of evening hat, silky and shiny . . . but he wore it almost all the time. It was a handy and safe place to put important things in.

Jimmy McGee had made everything that he wore. His coat had been made out of a piece of bombazine a tailor just threw out in the trash can. He had a cape, too, made of the same stuff, which he wore when he had work to do in the cellar of the opera house or way up in its round glass dome. There had been enough left over for him to make himself a regular work suit and this little hammock, in which he was now resting.

He'd also made a bombazine bag, which he slung over his shoulder to put found things in when they wouldn't go in his hat. It had a drawstring so you could pull it tightly together. This drawstring was made from leather and probably was a shoestring once used by some mountain climber in his sturdy footgear. And he had a little leather belt with brass studs on which he hung his tools when they didn't fit in the bag. The leather belt was probably from a little girl's roller skates. Maybe Amy's? He was like a miniature walking hardware store.

He also had a piece of bombazette, a more delicate fabric than bombazine, that he'd garnered from the same tailor shop. This finery he had stored in a piece of pipe all its own for some future unknown need.

But now, resting in his bombazine hammock, he felt the time had come for him to study this little book he had saved for Amy so it would not be soaked by fog or dew. It was a strange book. Though it always opened itself up to the M page, the book was in splendid ABC order, the way Jimmy McGee liked things to be. He himself kept his nuts and bolts in their proper bins arranged neatly and according to size and shape. So this book of Amy's was the way he liked to have things. But why did it always pop open to the M page?

This was a baffler. And yes, he saw his name again..."McGee, Jimmy: a little fellow, a plumber, a banger on pipes, a HERO!" That's why he was lying in his hammock and why he couldn't go drowsily off to sleep the way Amy and Clarissa had. All that Amy said about him in her book was true except the hero part of it. Where'd Amy ever get an idea like that about him?

He closed the book, but it wouldn't stay closed. Opened itself up all the time to the M page as though that page—it was page 13—said, "Read me!"

"Hero!"

This was more than a little unsettling to

Jimmy McGee. To take his mind off this hero business, he sprang up, slung his bombazine bag over his shoulder, and went off on his regular nighttime affairs. Soon the Cape Codder would be puffing by with the cod and the lobsters, the catch of the day, on its way to Boston. He had to shoo the cats and the dogs and even, now and then, a cow out of the way. So, off he went, for all of this work was part of his real business along with pipes and plumbing. Leave hero work to heroes...leave him out of it.

Then he returned to headquarters. He parted his fluttery curtains. The Amy book was still there, right in his hammock where he had left it, flipped open right to the M page. Might as well call it the Jimmy McGee page.

He scrutinized this page to see what company he was with. The name above his was:

Lydia, Little: a teeny, tiny doll with bright blue eyes, a do-nothing doll. Can't walk, can't talk, can't say "Mama." Has bristly, curly, long golden hair. Named after Lydia, Big.

In the book Lydia, Big, was above Lydia, Little.

Lydia, Big: Can do all the things Lydia, Little, can't do. Too big to bring to Truro. It was Bear or her. Bear won.

There were no N's on this page. But there was an empty space under McGee, Jimmy. Maybe Amy left it empty on purpose for the occasion when he really might become a hero and say how that came about?

All these things were confusing to Jimmy McGee, who was used to everything going along in an orderly way, not the way things were now, suddenly finding himself with the word *hero* attached to his name in a *Who's Who Book*! And with that blank space beneath him. Why?

That night he did his work in zoomie-zoomie-zoomie time—that means three times faster than usual. It wasn't easy work either. There was trouble in the electric bolt box in the cellar of a motion picture house—the lights kept coming on and going off right in the middle of the best part of the show. In spite of much stomping from the outraged people above him, he fixed everything and then returned to headquarters.

He took off his bombazine coat, folded it neatly, and put it at the foot of his hammock.

He put Amy's book inside his stovepipe hat, which was the safest place for it, and kept his hat on his head. Sometimes he hung his hat on a hatrack, a tough root near his hammock, where he could grab it in a hurry. Not tonight, though. His hat with this book in it was going to stay on top of his head until bright morning sunshine, when he'd put the *Who's Who Book* back on the bench.

He sat down in his entranceway and repeated the words in that Amy book. "McGee, Jimmy: a little fellow..." All of it, ending with "HERO."

He said the words over and over again so often that they made him laugh. They were like the lines in a play. "Ha-ha!" He surprised himself, laughing like that. "That *Who's Who* girl has gotten the wrong idea of me...that's the trouble. I'll think of something else, maybe some of the other people in the book. You can't think of yourself all the time...that's vain! I'll study the book, learn it by heart..."

A lovely breeze rustled the grass above and behind him. The moon was high, and its path sent silver ripples across the sea on the waves rolling in, way down below. Try as he did, though, the word *hero* would not get itself out of his head.

Just thinking about how you get to be a hero was hard enough, let alone already being labeled one. He liked hard work, was used to it, but he was not used to the idea of being a hero. He wondered if he *had* to be one just because Amy said so in her book. Still, he sort of wished he could keep this book he was in.

Sitting in his doorway, Jimmy McGee began to study the clouds—the moon, the stars, the planets—and watched them slowly move across the heavens. He learned a lot this way. He knew that toward the end of summer there would be a hurricane and the name of it would be Lobelia. He knew these things long before regular weather forecasters did.

At hurricane time he always had plenty to do! Lobelia. He liked the sound of it, a really pretty name for a hurricane, and might bring some curious surprise along with it besides wind and rain and tidal waves! And the name would fit right on the same page in Amy's book as his own hero name did. There was an empty space there, empty as though it were saying, "Write me a name here."

O.K. That he would do! He took the book out of his hat, and by the light of the pale early dawn, in his tiny scrawl, he wrote Lobelia.

His writing looked like marks left by a little bird. This amused him. It would give Amy something to puzzle about. Just even things up; like her having given him all this hero business to puzzle about.

Today was going to be a beautiful day, the first day of vacation for Amy and her family in The Bizzy Bee. Soon the sun would rise. He must put Amy's book back where he had found it when the bench was good and dry. She would never know that her book had spent the night in the stovepipe hat of a character in her book by the name of McGee, Jimmy ... hero.

He was reluctant to part with Amy's book, so he went inside his headquarters, and by the light of the early dawn seeping through his grass curtains, he made a copy of Amy's book to keep for himself. He had a nook where he kept scraps of paper he gathered from a newspaper printing shop down Provincetown way. So now he had his own copy of Amy's *Who's Who Book.*

He had several books written in his tiny script, a kind of code. He kept each book rolled up tightly in its own piece of pipe. They were his "scrolls" ... a pipe library, which he arranged neatly in a back corner of his cave. This was his summer library. He had another "scroll-pipe library" back in his Washington, D.C., winter headquarters.

A learned little plumber, this tiny Jimmy McGee was. But hero?

Sitting there quietly, not going on his rounds, he mulled over this hero business and mulled over it. Took his mind off his real work. But he had to figure it out, what Amy meant. He figured there were three kinds of heroes, the long-ago kind, the present-day kind, and the future kind, the hero-to-be kind.

He mused. "Ah!" he pondered. "Maybe, just maybe, mind you, maybe in some long ago past time, long, long ago, I once *was* a hero, and I have forgotten about it...if I ever knew it then when it was happening. Or, hey! Maybe there is, *maybe* I'm saying, another Jimmy McGee that I never heard of but Amy has? Some hero of long ago. Maybe I was named after him, a sort of fellow who always gets himself put into books by other people, say a book with a name like *Stories of Famous People.* Or the little boy who held his finger in a hole in the dike so the town would not get flooded if the dam burst. He probably didn't know he was being a hero and soon would be in books practically all over the world."

Or take a hero of more recent times, who gets

to have streets and boulevards named after him and a statue of him on a horse in Central Park or some park somewhere, maybe, or in a museum, or in a little garden outside the museum with a fountain splashing water all over him all the time. Like himself, for instance, behind his waterfall in Mount Rose Park?

Or maybe a hero so recent he has ticker-tape parades down Fifth Avenue or Constitution Avenue, people clapping, shouting, roaring, "Hail! Hail!"

Or maybe Amy meant that he, Jimmy McGee, would be a hero in the near future. He had better keep his eyes out for that chance happening to bring Amy's book up to date. But not to let all this hero business interfere with his real work. "No! Never!"

The sun was not yet high enough for him to risk putting Amy's valuable book back where she had left it. The bench was still damp. Perhaps some seagull—they are curious birds, think everything they see is possibly good to eat, something novel, and squawk and scream over it—might fly off with it in its sharp beak to Gull Island or even Provincetown, scattering shredded pages of Amy's *Who's Who Book*, including the important L and M page, all over the ocean.

He couldn't risk that. Amy wouldn't be out of bed yet anyway. He had taken good care of her book and wanted to see her delight at finding it safe and sound; all he had done that was extra was to have added a little something for fun!

So he popped it in his bombazine bag. Then he zoomie-zoomied off to make his morning rounds, waking people up...the ones who had to get to work early. Check the milk train. Was it on time? Slow? Check the switches. *The Boston Globe,* was it on the train? Well, all the usual morning chores. He went faster than ever, making the telephone wires hum, gathering extra electric speed, because he wanted to return Amy's book, which was bumping about in his bombazine bag along with a very special little box, about two inches long and one inch high and wide, an oblong very strong little box. This he always carried with him. It was what he was going to put two special bolts in some day. He called it the magic bolt box.

He had a good collection of bolts all right, but something was lacking. Then one day an idea, like a bolt out of the blue, had struck him. For a long time he had had a longing to have a thunderbolt and a lightning bolt represented in his collection. Perhaps he could capture in his box the tiny, very, very small tip end of a lightning bolt and the last rumble of a thunderbolt.

To try to capture these rare items for his bolt collection would help him forget the hero business. As far as his chores went, all was fine. All trains on time. No dogs hurt, no cats either, no little slowpoke hedgehog run over. Pipes everywhere, all O.K. All were banged on louder than ever, shuddering the cottages and shaking the people out of their beds.

The sun was up. He zoomie-zoomied back to his summer headquarters in six-sixty time. He went so fast he might have passed himself coming back! That was how curious he was about Amy's book. It was hard for him to part with it, but he was not a book thief or any other kind of thief. He placed the book on the bench in the sweet morning sunshine. It opened automatically to the M page. Though the breeze fluttered the pages, back they always came to the M page. This was a baffler!

Jimmy McGee got back to his headquarters just in the nick of time. Amy and Clarissa, still dressed in their nightgowns, barefooted—he hadn't even banged their pipes yet—tore over to the bench at the top of the twenty-six steps. "Shows how valuable that book is!" thought Jimmy McGee. "Something magic about it, maybe..."

He postponed finishing his usual business and stayed behind the lacy grass curtains of his headquarters and listened.

"Ah-ah," breathed Amy. "It's safe and sound. Opens as always to the M page. And you know who's on that page, don't you?"

"Why, Jimmy McGee, of course," said Clarissa. "But, Amy, what are all those funny-looking smudges below McGee, Jimmy, in that empty space there?" she demanded.

Amy looked closely. "Well, those are probably the footprints of some curious gull or an adventuresome sandpiper who made it up the twenty-six steps. I'm not 'sprized. At the beach anything can happen."

Amy smelled her book. "Smells like stove polish," she said, laughing. "Book! Have you been on adventures in the night? Like the midnight ride of Paul Revere?"

Clarissa laughed. Amy went on. "It's lucky I

had written in the front, 'If this book should chance to roam, bring it back to Amy's home. Reward. No questions asked.'"

"That person saw that and brought it back and didn't wait for the reward," said Clarissa.

"We will bring a pancake out for him. That will be his reward for honesty. But come on in because it is pancakes for breakfast. I smell them."

"Smell better than stove polish," said Clarissa.

Amy hugged her little book. "I love you, book!" she said. "And I'm glad you're safe and sound. And I like the smell of stove polish."

Amy and Clarissa went in. Jimmy McGee heard all that talk. And he heard the last words before the screen door slammed behind them. Amy said, "After pancakes, we'll put on our bathing suits, go down to the beach, and we'll make sand castles."

Clarissa clapped her hands and jumped up and down. "Oh!" she cried. "I never have done that before in all my borned life!"

"We'll take Little Lydia," said Amy. "She's never seen the ocean either. We will make a castle for her, just for her."

"And," said Clarissa sternly, "Amy, you must leave your *Who's Who Book* in The Bizzy Bee!"

"Yes," said Amy. "I will tuck it under the mattress. Even Wags won't know where I hid it."

"Yes," agreed Clarissa. "Because maybe it *is* magic, opening up all the time to the same page."

And they went into The Bizzy Bee. Jimmy McGee heard that the screen door squeaked and thought he should fix it when no one was around. He could smell the bacon and the pancakes. But none of these things interested him now. What interested him now was this Lydia, Little, business.

He got his scroll copy of the *Who's Who Book* out of its pipe and read, "Lydia, Little: a teeny, tiny doll with bright blue eyes, a do-nothing doll."

"Well," thought Jimmy McGee, "soon I will see this Little Lydia doll." So he postponed his next rounds until after he had gotten a glimpse of her. What he wondered was this: Was there a connection between him and Little Lydia? "No," he answered himself. "A happenstance. Just the correct place in the alphabet for the two of us." He was Number 13 in the alphabet.

She was Number 12. Still he mulled over this coincidence.

Was it tied up in any way with McGee, Jimmy...a hero? Is that what Amy knew about and he didn't?

He should go out now on his rounds, do his work. But then Amy and Clarissa with towels and pails and shovels came out of The Bizzy Bee. Amy had some little thing clutched tightly in her fist. Might it be Little Lydia? The teeny, tiny doll? The do-nothing doll?

He had to wait and see. It might be Little Lydia. "If it is, I must wait and get a real good look at her," Jimmy McGee thought. "After all, in the book we're on the same page. In real life our paths may cross...I must wait and see and be ready."

He tapped his stovepipe hat and sat down in his doorway and watched.

3

Lydia, Little,
a Do-Nothing Doll

Amy and Clarissa, dressed in their bathing suits—Clarissa's was red, Amy's blue—with all their paraphernalia—towels, pails, shovels, Little Lydia in Amy's tight little fist—practically flew down the twenty-six steps.

"They'd be good at the zoomie-zoomies," thought Jimmy McGee in admiration. He waited to see where they were going to set up their beach headquarters.

They stopped right below Jimmy McGee's headquarters, not too far from the steps, not too near the ocean, close enough to the steep dune to get some shade from the afternoon sun. It was a perfect spot for them, and a good one for Jimmy McGee to take in all the goings-on from behind his lacy sea-grass curtain high above them under the edge of the dune.

It was Little Lydia he was most interested in right now. Here was the real Lydia, Little, the one who was on the same page as he was in the *Who's Who Book* by Amy. Of course, this made a sort of connection between them. It might even be a clue as to why Amy chose to add hero to her definition of him in her book.

Amy said, as she spread out their towels, "This is a good place, Clarissa, not too near the high-water line and near the shade of the dune. Besides, other people will not be stepping all over us on their way to and fro. Do you see any horseshoe crabs?"

"I don't know," said Clarissa. "This is my very first day at the ocean. And I didn't know crabs wore horseshoes!"

"Well, I don't see any," said Amy. "They're big, Clarissa. But they don't bite, Papa says. Still, how do we know whether or not one of them might mistake Little Lydia for a rare fish, make off with her, capture her and keep her in prison under his hard brown shell?"

"I don't see anything of that sort," said

Clarissa. "All I see is ocean, sand...oh, how beautiful it is here!"

"Yes!" agreed Amy. "And now we must show Little Lydia the sights!"

Amy picked Little Lydia up. She held her high above her head. "Breathe!" she said. But Little Lydia was a do-nothing doll. So naturally she didn't breathe, or blink, or say, "My goodness!" But her face had a pretty smile painted on it, and her eyes were as blue as the sea and the sky, so you would think they could see! The little dress she had on was of calico. It had a blue background with tiny little pink roses in its pattern. She was made of rubber so that she could sit or be put in any position.

"Pretty, very pretty," thought Jimmy McGee. So *that* was Little Lydia, the do-nothing doll with electric blue eyes that stared at the sky!

"We're going to make a castle for you," Amy told Little Lydia. "A sand castle, and more than just that. You'll see." She carefully laid Little Lydia down on the tiny blue shawl that she had crocheted for her, and she and Clarissa started on their construction.

Jimmy McGee watched them bring pails of

water and pat the sand down firmly. About to leave to do his work, he took a last look at Little Lydia. A slight breeze had changed her position, so she was lying a little more on her side. Instead of staring at the sky, her electric blue eyes were now riveted directly on him!

Jimmy McGee rubbed his own eyes. "Am I seeing things?" It was as though Little Lydia could see through his grassy curtains and watch him.

"Nonsense!" he told himself. "A do-nothing doll is a do-nothing doll. She can't see with those electric blue eyes of hers, not me or anything else. But, bye!" he said in bebop code language. This was his own language that he had developed during his miles and miles of zoomie-zoomie traveling over electric telephone wires, train tracks, trollies, everywhere. So far as he knew, he was the only one who knew the language. But he had made a dictionary of this bebop code. It was in one of his scrolls, and he kept it in his language division.

Off he went now in six-sixty time. And Amy and Clarissa went about their business of creating a castle with rooms in it and a moat around it and turrets on top as a watch-out place for visitors, be they horseshoe crabs or whatever! Some unknown enemy! This was going to be Little Lydia's headquarters.

Now and then Jimmy McGee came back, curious himself, to see how things were going in the making of the castle. But he stayed only long enough to see the foundations being laid or a bedroom added. Then he would be off again. Sometimes, far away, he would hear the rumbling of thunder, and he'd head off in that direction! He always hoped that *this* time, during *this* storm, he would capture the tiny tip end of a lightning bolt and the final rumble of a thunderbolt, pop them in his tough little strong box saved for this very purpose. What a way to round out his already amazing collection of nuts and bolts that would be!

At first he had called his empty little box "the magic bolt box." Then he thought he might change the name to his "thunder and lightning bolt box" or even to the "bolt-out-of-the-blue box." He'd see what fitted in best when he caught these precious bolts and how he used them. He meant, if he ever did catch them, to use them for some, so far unknown, special occasion. Until then, he would always carry them in their safety box inside his stovepipe hat.

But he missed out on that storm. It petered out before he could get there even in his fast zoomie-zoomie-zoomie time.

Now, back at the beach, he saw that Amy and Clarissa were having a more successful time of it. They were creating a miraculous castle. Patting down the sand here, shaping it there, they formed rooms, a big hall, a banquet room, and a bedroom. They had propped Little Lydia up

now against a fragile wisp of sea grass, fluttering slightly in the gentle summer breeze, where
she could watch what was going on solely for
her, the creation of Little Lydia's castle!

A sand castle with a moat and a drawbridge,
all for Little Lydia, a do-nothing doll, but a
princess now, with a castle all her own. By the
end of the day Amy and Clarissa were pretty
tired. They laid Little Lydia on the couch they
had patted down for her in her big bedroom.

"Should we leave her here all night and let
her listen to the swishing sound of the waves

rolling in on time, rolling out on time?" Amy wondered.

"And hear the peepers up and down Cape Cod as though they were singing a concert, a lullaby concert?" added Clarissa.

"A lullaby for Little Lydia, stargazing," said Amy.

Soon the sun would set. Little Lydia would be lying there, gazing and gazing at the sky, blue eyes wide open all the time. Amy said, "You know, Clarissa, there is no roof to this palace. Little Lydia might get lonely. And there is no prince, no one to guard her. I think we should take her into The Bizzy Bee in the nighttime."

Clarissa agreed. "Yes. Much safer inside. Out here maybe a big bad monster, not a prince in white armor, might capture her."

"M-m-m," said Amy. "Each night we'll bring her in, and each morning bring her back out. Tomorrow we'll build a little town all stretching out beyond her castle, nestling at the foot of the dune. It could have little streets and houses."

"Oh, yes!" said Clarissa happily.

"And we could make little people out of hard sand," Amy went on.

"Oh, yes," said Clarissa, laughing. "And little peepers might come and live in the castle, keep Little Lydia company, and in the houses, too. Be pets for the little children!"

They picked Little Lydia up gently, brushed the sand out of her fluffy golden hair, and went in to dinner. Later Amy felt under the mattress for her book. It was there and safe. It didn't pop open to the L and M page. Being under the mattress may have cured it of that curious habit. She put it on her pillow with Little Lydia on top of it, so both were safe and sound.

Then, because it was such a star-studded night, Papa suggested they should all go out and look at the sky. Papa knew a great deal about the heavens and pointed out the constellations. Now they all knew how to locate the North Star and Cassiopeia's Chair and a great deal besides. They then began to look for and count the shooting stars.

"There goes one!" exclaimed Amy.

"Oh! I missed that one," said Clarissa. "Oh-oh! But there goes another one!"

Sometimes one of them saw a star streak across the sky, sometimes someone else did. It was a game. They began to keep track.

"There's one," said Amy.

"Oh! I missed it," said Mama.

By the time they went in, it was practically a tie. Amy and Clarissa had each seen four, Papa three, Mama, not sure, thought only two. "It's my eyes!" said Mama.

Then it was time for bed. Amy tied the little hand-crocheted blue shawl she had made for Little Lydia from one iron post to the next at the foot of the bed. Amy's *Who's Who Book* was to be Little Lydia's mattress. But what do you know? The minute Amy laid it in the hammock, it sprang open, as it always used to, to the L and M page.

Amy closed it firmly, put an elastic band around it, and laid Little Lydia on top of it. "That will straighten you out, book!" she said. When Wags came in—he always checked on everybody—he poked the little hammock gently with his big paw and set it gently rocking.

Amy and Clarissa got into the bed they shared. The evenings were cool here in Truro. They snuggled under the warm, puffy comforter Mama put over them when she kissed them good night. "Go to sleep now, you two," she said. "Tomorrow is another day." Then she tiptoed out of the room as though they were already asleep.

They talked a little, in very soft voices, so Mama would think they really were asleep.

Clarissa whispered, "What do you think the piper, Jimmy McGee, is doing now? I mean the pipe man, the plumber, the banger-on-pipes man."

"Sh-sh-sh," whispered Amy. "I'm thinking... thinking... Tomorrow is... another..."

"Day," finished Clarissa.

Both fell asleep to the exultant song of the peepers, rising louder and louder, an accompaniment to the lovely sound of the great waves of the ocean rolling in, breaking, and then rolling back.

As for Jimmy McGee, what was he doing? He, too, had been watching the shooting stars. But mainly he was musing about an idea he had, a nice one, that had to do with Little Lydia's sand castle.

This idea was more in his line of work, plumbing mainly, than aiming to somehow become a hero. He put the smallest tools he owned in his stovepipe hat. In the moonlight, he zoomie-zoomied down and stood beside the sand castle of Little Lydia. He had in mind to add his own touch to this pretty castle in the sand. How? What? Well…he hadn't decided yet. Maybe a drawbridge that would really go up, go down?

In the end he did nothing. After all, this castle was the creation of Amy and Clarissa. He could admire it, but he could not put the Jimmy McGee touch on it. But wait. In his "found things" he remembered he had picked up a fragile, tiny piece of a child's silver chain. He laid it beside the moat, where he supposed the drawbridge would go. It could be part of the equipment for that. Help it go up and go down. Maybe Amy and Clarissa would think of that and use it that way, or use it any way they wanted.

Then off he went on his rounds.

In the morning, Amy and Clarissa did see the little piece of chain. Instead of using it for their drawbridge, they looped it around Little Lydia's neck. "Now the princess has some jewels," said Amy.

All up and down the beach other children were now building sand castles...a long row of castles and palaces. Amy and Clarissa were busily creating their little princess's town, her townspeople, a pavilion for a concert. Wags was always beside them, having scraped the hot sand on top off until he reached cool, damp sand below, on which he would lie and then watch Amy and Clarissa or doze. Mama and Papa were talking and chatting and laughing with old friends a little ways away. Much laughter everywhere. And so one day slipped into the next, and many days went gently by.

Little Lydia, reigning princess over a vast domain, seemed oblivious to all of this. But somehow, no matter how Amy had placed her, no matter how the wind was blowing, her position always seemed to change so that her electric blue eyes became riveted on the top of the dune where Jimmy McGee had his headquarters. Could they penetrate through his lacy curtains?

Jimmy McGee made note of this and vaguely wondered. But he had other matters still to ponder. One, of course, was why hero? And the other was where, how, and when he could capture the tiny tip end of a lightning bolt and the rumble-rolling last sound of its thunderbolt. These were hard nuts to crack.

At the top of the dune
By the light of the moon
Jim, Little McGee,
May be writing a tune
Like a strange ancient rune
That sings the odd tale of
What will happen some
Afternoon soon...
Soon—very soon!

4

Monstrous

Every day when Jimmy McGee came home from his rounds, it made him happy always to see Little Lydia, that do-nothing doll, lying below him in her splendid sand castle gazing straight up at him at the top of the dune. He was glad to have something else to think about besides the hero business.

He wished he could think of something that would turn a do-nothing doll into a wide-awake, do-something doll. She was prettier than ever with the delicate, fragile necklace around her neck, sparkling in the sunshine.

Now it was early in the morning, and it was business as usual for him today. He slung his bombazine bag over his shoulder, clamped his stovepipe hat on his head, and shook his head to make certain his sturdy magic bolt box was bumping around up there, all ready for the tiny tail end of a lightning bolt and the last rumble of a thunderbolt to round out his collection of nuts and bolts. "Oh, let this be that day," he prayed, "for the capture of those bolts!"

First he zoomie-zoomied over to The Bizzy Bee to wake up the people there. He gave the pipes such a mighty thwack that the whole house shuddered. Then off he went on his rounds, having made a chart in his mind as to towns most likely to have a thunderstorm that day. As he left, he heard Amy's joyous voice.

"Get up! Get up! Mama! Papa! Clarissa! Wags! Get up!" she said.

Amy hated to stay in bed with all that ocean out there and with Little Lydia's castle and its surrounding town. She had to get up! Clarissa was impatient, too. As for Wags, he tore to the screen door and scratched at it, banging his beautiful big head against it because he heard the milk train and was anxious to get out. He wanted to chase it if he could, "woof" at it, scare it so that it would go away and never come back.

Amy and Clarissa began to bounce on the springy, creaky double-size iron bed they shared. Higher and higher they bounced and sometimes bumped each other's head. "Ouch! Ouch!" they screamed and collapsed limply on the soft bedcovers only to begin again, bouncing and chanting, "It's time to get up! It's time to get up, get up, get up 'cause it's morning!"

"Jumping jacks!" said Mama.

Finally Mama and Papa got themselves up and stood dressing and yawning marvelously. Papa's yawn could be heard in the next town probably. Mama filled the teakettle, made the coffee, and started the oatmeal. Amy and Clarissa splashed water on their faces and made plans for the day.

"We'll take Little Lydia to the beach. She can watch us make a little schoolroom, with children sitting in it. And we'll put a flat piece of driftwood over the moat, even if there isn't any water in it...might rain, you know."

She picked Little Lydia up. She said, "Lydia, Little! You know you are a princess, Princess Lydia of Sand Castle Number One, at the foot of the dune. Princesses are always captured or have a spell cast over them. You may be captured by some Monstrous something. But, don't worry! Someone will rescue you."

Amy and Clarissa had a wonderful day. They found a flat piece of driftwood and laid it across the moat for a drawbridge. "People will have to walk across it," said Amy.

"There should be water," complained Clarissa.

"People have to 'magine something," said Amy indignantly.

"I was only thinking of what you said," Clarissa explained. "I didn't want some Monstrous something to just plain walk across a board and grab Little Lydia."

"M-m-m," said Amy. "But, come on. We're going to make a little schoolroom, remember? And little kids to sit in little sand chairs... remember?"

"Yes," said Clarissa.

They moved down to the part of the sand town where they had built a little sand school, with desks, but no children in it yet. But Amy said, "Ooooh!"

"What?" asked Clarissa.

"Look how dark it's getting. There's going to be a squall!" said Amy. "We'd better gather up our toys and towels."

Amy's mother came to the top of the twenty-six steps and said, "Children, come in! There's going to be a squall, I think."

Amy handed her things to Clarissa and said, "Hold mine for a minute. I want to show Little Lydia a big wave. She's always lying there on her couch in her castle. So far she's never even seen a huge wave. We won't go very close..."

Amy ran as close to the water as was safe, she thought. She held Little Lydia in her outstretched hands. "See? Little Lydia? Monstrous big wave!"

And this wave *was* truly Monstrous. Amy backed off in a hurry. In doing so, she dropped Little Lydia, and the big wave rolled in and grabbed her and tossed her around in its lacy froth and rolled back to sea, where it began to gather force for the next big splash on the beach.

But Little Lydia was gone! She was not riding in on the next, or the next wave. No sign of her. The tide was turning, going out, the waves receding and leaving no Little Lydia behind. She was gone.

Amy and Clarissa stood there by Little Lydia's castle. Somehow, Amy thought, Monstrous may

have a kind heart and whisk her back over the sand to her home? No. Not so. They went up to the bench at the top of the stairs, where they sat in stunned silence.

Mama came out to see that Amy and Clarissa were coming up to The Bizzy Bee. "No need to come in now," she said, "if you don't want to. This is a funny storm." Half the sky, far away, was still sunny. The other half, this side, was still the deep dark purple the sky gets before a storm. "I think the storm will bypass us," she said, and she went back inside The Bizzy Bee. "No need to run around closing windows, anyway."

And this was true, for now the sun burst through the dark clouds and it was as though the squall had never been around these parts ever. Except that now they did not have Little Lydia. She was riding the waves somewhere. As they wiped the sand off their feet, tears crept down Amy's cheek. They talked about Monstrous.

Jimmy McGee zoomied back from his fruit-less search at this moment. He had not had the good fortune to track down a single thunder-storm where it might have been possible for him to catch his treasured bolts. No thunderbolt, no lightning bolt yet in his special strong box. He sat down in his doorway and listened to the conversation taking place on the little bench at the top of the stairs.

Amy and Clarissa looked woebegone, but talked excitedly as people do when an out-of-the-ordinary event has taken place. Amy was acting something out, waving her arms about, holding a pretend something in her little hands, then stretching them out for something to where, and for what? Now and then she wiped her eyes. Clarissa handed her her towel to wipe them.

Jimmy McGee listened carefully. He took off his hat and put the little safety bolt box into one of his back vaults, its special place when it was not in his hat or his bombazine bag. He put his hat back on, returned to his "front porch," and from behind its lacy curtains heard this:

AMY: Poor Little Lydia! Lost! Drowned!

CLARISSA: Maybe we'll find her tomorrow. Maybe another big wave will toss her back on the beach, maybe right into her own castle! On her own couch!

AMY: Been eaten by a fish, maybe, or... well...something Monstrous did grab her!

CLARISSA: O-o-oh! The Monstrous thing you were talking about?

AMY: Yes! The Monstrous wave was that thing! I should'a hung on to her and backed away sooner and faster.

CLARISSA: Yes! That's it! It was that very same Monstrous that grabbed her up and swirled her away! I'm glad Pee-Wee didn't get grabbed by Monstrous! She's my only doll.

AMY: But Little Lydia is my only Little Lydia! So cute. With that frizzy golden hair they put on her head, not a wig, but as though it had grown there naturally. And those blue eyes, electric blue, I'd call them. Did you ever notice that, Clarissa?

CLARISSA: No, Amy. But now I think of it, I think you are right. But could we go in, Amy? I'm shivering. Are my lips blue?

AMY: Blue, yes. We'll go in. But first I have to write something in my *Who's Who Book.* (Amy took her book out of her beach-coat pocket.)

CLARISSA: How are you going to write something out here without a pencil?

AMY: I keep a pencil in this crack between these two boards. There it is. My blue pencil. (And Amy wrote something in her book.)

CLARISSA: What did you write, Amy, in your book that I'm in and also out of, and Pee-Wee, and...

AMY: Next to "Lydia, Little: a teeny, tiny doll with bright blue eyes, a do-nothing doll. Can't walk, can't talk, can't say 'Mama.' Has bristly, curly, long golden hair. Named after Lydia, Big," I added, "Lost in the ocean. Captured by a Monstrous wave!"

CLARISSA: That makes it real, to put it in the book like that! Now you'll never find her.

AMY: Wait! I have added something else: "But I hope she will be rescued by a Hero!"

CLARISSA: You did say in your *Who's Who Book* under McGee, Jimmy, "HERO." So maybe he will be the one who will rescue her. It's funny about that book. Maybe it is magic. Once you thought you wouldn't find it, but then you did...even after leaving it out all night!

AMY: Someone found it, probably read it, then put it back, an honest person, not like some crooks. Just didn't wash his hands. Smudges still here. (Two tears were finding their way down Amy's cheek.)

CLARISSA (taking Amy's hand in hers): I bet we'll find her tomorrow when the tide comes in...all the way in. She may roll in with it. So don't be sad...

AMY: I hope so. Oh-h, I hope so. She's like a little princess. I'll put Bear at the foot of the hammock in the front yard, looking out to sea, like the captain of a ship, the *S.S. Bizzy Bee.* On the lookout for lost Little Lydia. Oh! And remember! She is made of rubber, and rubber floats. She may be having a good time.

In this way Amy tried to cheer herself up, and that was the end of the conversation. Amy and Clarissa, arms around each other's shoulders, went into The Bizzy Bee.

And Jimmy McGee went back inside his headquarters. He pondered about all that he had overheard. Especially, he pondered Amy's latest entry in her book. He'd have to bring his scroll copy up to date. "But I hope she will be rescued by a Hero!"

There was that word again...hero. Under his name and now also under Lydia, Little. He lay down in his bombazine hammock to think about this. Hero? Him?

5

The Rescue

Sitting in the doorway of his headquarters, Jimmy McGee mulled over all that he had overheard Amy and Clarissa say. This time Amy had not left anything like the book behind her. But she had left words that echoed and echoed in Jimmy McGee's mind.

"Lydia, Little...a do-nothing doll....Lost in the ocean. Captured by a Monstrous wave! But I hope she will be rescued by a Hero!"

There was that word again, always that problem, hero! In Amy's *Who's Who Book* he, Jimmy McGee, was labeled a hero. Now the word hero was on Little Lydia's line in the book, the line right before his. Was there a connection? There might be!

Jimmy McGee went to his library and took

his bebop code copy of Amy's *Who's Who Book* out of its scroll pipe to bring it up to date. Next to Lydia, Little, he scratched in the words, "Lost in the ocean. Captured by a Monstrous wave! But I hope she will be rescued by a Hero!" Who would that hero be? Perhaps...probably...he himself. And he put the scroll back in its proper scroll pipe.

Perhaps Amy could predict the making of a hero out of an ordinary plumber, the way he could predict storms and hurricanes and hot spells or cold. This thought satisfied him. So now all he had to do was to fulfill a prediction, that made by a little girl named Amy who had chosen to include him in her book of names along with her mama and her papa and her friends and dolls and the great dog Wags...and also Bear. There he was propped right above him in Amy's hammock, a watcher of the sea by day and by night. A teddy bear captain, looking for Little Lydia. He should have binoculars.

Not to let this prediction of Amy's interfere with his work, that was the important thing. Be a hero on the side...his sideline. The trouble was he had very little time for hobbies and sidelines and fulfilling other people's predictions. Especially now, at the height of summer, with Hurricane Lobelia coming in late August, according to his predictions.

Think of all the work a plumber, a banger on pipes, had to do then...getting people out of their houses if Lobelia decided to come to Cape Cod, helping them close up their cottages, not to forget to turn off the tap in their cellars. Does that seem to allow much time for sidelines?

"And don't forget," he reminded himself, "that my main aim, no sideline to this, is the capture of the tiny tip end of a lightning bolt and the final rumble of the thunderbolt!" Sometime soon he must catch these important bolts. Tiny they would have to be, but big as a whale in his mind. He smiled. Big as Monstrous! He laughed out loud. He liked hard work. Two big jobs! Rescuing Little Lydia and rounding out his nuts-and-bolts collection!

Tonight there was a full moon. This meant that the tide would be especially high. Already the waves were quite high. Many summer people down on the beach, taking advantage of one of the lovely evenings of late summer, were having barbecues, but would soon begin to get ready to go in. The smell of hot dogs and hamburgers lingered in the air. Jimmy McGee enjoyed the sound of laughter, the high-pitched sounds of the ladies, the sudden outbursts of the men, the squeals of delight of the children. But soon, all was quiet. Just the smell of the smoking embers was all that was left.

Amy's family had long since gone in, and the two little girls were probably in bed. The tide had not shifted yet, and the light of the moon made the sea rosy-hued or a deep violet, ever changing, ever beautiful. The wet sand mirrored these colors, so sea and sky melted together in the moonlight.

Often on such nights Jimmy McGee found good lost things, some nut or some bolt, a strange piece of driftwood, and would sling these in his bombazine bag to take back to headquarters. But tonight he had something different on his mind.

Because of the full moon, the tide was now coming in closer and faster. Some children, who had built their castles too close to the high-water mark, would find that theirs had melted in the waves. Not Amy and Clarissa's, though. They and many other children had been smart to build their castles close to the dune. So Little Lydia's castle and her little town were going to be safe, not swept away when the waves rolled in closer and closer.

Jimmy McGee took note of all this. He said to himself, "Suppose that tonight I should rescue Little Lydia as I am supposed to do according to the book? Would that make me a hero? Of course. Rescued by Jimmy McGee! Rescued from Monstrous! That would be the end of all of this hero-to-be business and could be labeled 'Business done!' Then I could forget it, put Little Lydia back on her couch, and I could get back to my nuts and bolts and my banging on pipes....

"Hey! But I'm way ahead of myself. Little Lydia is still somewhere in the ocean blue. Lucky she is made of rubber, except for her frizzy hair. I must be on the alert."

Jimmy McGee zoomied down to the beach. Now the tide was nearly high, the waves swelling and roiling way up on the beach, edging up to where he was standing. He backed off. Taking his stovepipe hat off his head, he emptied it of its nuts and bolts close to the dune, behind Little Lydia's castle.

Now, hat empty, Jimmy McGee went back to the nearest but safest edge of the incoming waves. He was not a seafaring little man. He was a landlubber interested in cellars and mainly in banging pipes. Still, he was brave and wanted to fulfill Amy's prediction about him, if possible...and end that hero business.

What chance would a Little Lydia have in an ocean so vast and strong?

"Waves!" said Jimmy McGee. "Halt! Stop a minute. If one of you has a Little Lydia bobbing around on your chest, let her go! Please let her have a peaceful ride in, or..."

He could not finish. The next wave was tremendous, a giant wave! Monstrous! You would think it did not belong to the sea but had a life all its own and would rise higher and higher and even up and over the dune. That's how mon-

strous it was! Jimmy McGee backed up quickly. But he held his stovepipe hat straight out in front of him, like a beggar pleading for alms.

This monstrous wave seemed to stand still for a moment before hurling itself on shore. In that moment before it broke, Jimmy McGee saw a tiny object swirling and whirling in its frothy crest! Then it broke! As it did, it popped that tiny thing, whatever it was, right into Jimmy McGee's hat! Quick as a wink, he clapped his hat tightly on his head as the wave rolled back.

"Thank you," said Jimmy McGee. He retreated swiftly up to his headquarters, scooping

up his nuts and bolts on the way, and sat down in the doorway. He took off his hat cautiously, held it upside down, and peered in. By the light of the moon he saw what he had captured, a tiny doll in a sopping-wet flowered summer dress and with frizzy golden hair!

"Ah!" said Jimmy McGee. "You are Lydia, Little. I recognize you because I have seen you in your sand castle, a little princess, and watched Amy and Clarissa making you a town around your castle. You are in the L's right ahead of me in Amy's book."

Naturally, Little Lydia did not reply. He looked at her, straight into her electric blue eyes. Naturally, too, she did not blink. Even if you squeezed her, she couldn't say anything or blink.

"That's all right," said Jimmy McGee. "Don't let it worry you—not saying anything but seeing plenty! I've seen you in your castle, so I know it's you. I've been wanting to run a little pipe in there to bang on in case of trouble. It would be like a fire alarm, and the whole family would come running, grab you up and keep you safe inside. No more trouble with Monstrous or who knows what other danger?

"But right now, I've got my other work to do, and you'll have to come with me on my rounds.

Don't want to lose you or have some other Monstrous something catch hold of you. In the morning I'll lay you on your sand castle divan, and won't Amy be surprised?"

Before clapping his hat on—it was only a little wet—he took a long look at Little Lydia. He smiled. He liked her looks. She had a pretty smiling face; the paint had not washed off. Her hair was drying out and was all fluffed up like a movie star's. No wonder Amy had been sad losing such an odd little doll as this, a doll cut out for adventure.

Adventure! That's what she was going to have. Already had had Monstrous! Next, what?

He plunked her way up in his stovepipe hat, clamped it firmly on his head, and was about to take off when from far away he heard the rumble of distant thunder and saw the zigzags of lightning. That Lydia! She *had* taken his mind off his work. He had forgotten his precious little strong box, destined, he hoped, to have captured in it the tiny tip end of a streak of lightning and the faint last rumble of thunder. He lifted his stovepipe hat a fraction, shoved his little bolt box inside, and then clamped his hat back on very tightly.

Jimmy McGee had been so busy rescuing

Little Lydia, maybe making himself into a hero, that he had not been paying enough attention to his real work. He had not estimated just exactly where this storm that he was tracking down was centered. He listened intently. Ah, another rumble! He loved the sound of distant thunder. He loved close-up thunder, too. Bang! Bang! Bang! Like a mighty man banging on a mighty pipe! Right in his line of work, though his was on a modest scale. Lightning, too, he liked. That's probably why he moved like lightning... his zoomie-zoomies made him move with the speed of lightning. But, unlike lightning, his zoomie-zoomies never wore themselves out, nor hurt anything or anybody. They were magic. Even in Amy's *Who's Who Book* in the Z's it said, "Zoomie-zoomies: a magic that can make people who have it do curious things."

Well, now, on, he hoped, to the capture of the bolts!

6

The Magic Bolt Box

Jimmy McGee, on his six-sixty way to track down a storm he figured was down Ipswich way, or farther down the coast, was beginning to have a strong feeling that this might, *might,* mind you, be the very storm in which he could catch his special thunder and lightning bolts. He was feeling somewhat elated, self-confident, filled with electricity! Maybe it was because he had rescued Little Lydia. But he was beginning to think less and less of Little Lydia and more and more about the important task he had set for himself.

After all, he was not cut out to be a doll-rescuer and doll-minder. He was a plumber pure and simple. Call him hero or don't call him hero—it didn't matter to him, not right now anyway as he heard the thunder and saw, not too far away, streaks of lightning!

He was certain now, from the sound of the thunder and the speed of the lightning, that this storm was down Ipswich way, and he zoomied through the telephone wires and was soon there. By now the storm was passing on. Here were simply the final rumblings of thunder and slight flashes of lightning, as afterthoughts, a kind of gentle ending to the storm! As if saying to Jimmy McGee, "Want some? Take some before it is too late!"

He reached in his hat for his special little bolt box. He was very careful not to let Little Lydia slip out. Then he really did forget all about her!

In a little town very near to Ipswich, about one hundred and fifty miles from his summer headquarters, Jimmy McGee zoomie-zoomied to the top of a pretty church on the green there. He knew about this church. In one of his scrolls he had a record of where and how many times every little church had been struck by lightning, and this church had had its steeple struck by lightning three times. Lightning must love it. So there he stood at the very tiptop, poised and balanced on its pointed spire. He opened his little bolt box and stretched it out in front of him.

"Come on, thunder! Come on, lightning!" he challenged, while balancing himself and urgently hoping. His hopes were rewarded.

What happened next was exactly what had happened earlier in the evening in the rescue of Little Lydia from Monstrous!

He did capture with a sizzling ping-ping the tiny frail tail of a flash of lightning and the final rumble of the thunderbolt, a comforting sound. Both quieted down right away when Jimmy McGee locked them inside his little bolt box. They couldn't get out. He pressed the box into his stovepipe hat.

It was only because of his magic powers that Jimmy McGee was able to capture them. No one else in the world could do it or should even try... too dangerous!

He was elated. But he had completely forgotten the other occupant of his stovepipe hat, Little Lydia. At the moment all he thought about was what an awe-inspiring addition he had gotten to his rare collection of nuts and bolts, a large number of them odd ones from

many places and times. It was his intention never to let these new bolts loose until the absolutely right moment to do so came! What moment would that be? Some heroic moment?

Oh, my goodness! *Hero!* There was Little Lydia, sitting on a little box filled with thunder and lightning bolts on top of his head in his stovepipe hat! Or the box might be sitting on her! What must that seem like to Little Lydia?

He tried to reassure himself. "Remember," he said, "a do-nothing doll like Little Lydia wouldn't realize one thing about it."

Making sure that his hat was clamped down tightly, he zoomied back from the pretty church steeple to his summer headquarters. He did this in six-sixty time! He was as happy as he would have been had he captured a star!

He went inside and entered this adventure in one of his scrolls, the one labeled "Most Important Bolts," put it back in its pipe, put it in his library, and sat down in his doorway to think things over. Monstrous! And then thunder and lightning bolts! What a day!

But he did not have much time to relax, to think!

Strange sounds were coming from inside his stovepipe hat.

"Oh, my goodness!" Jimmy McGee exclaimed. "Little Lydia! Jogging around with thunder and lightning bolts, even though tiny, inside my stovepipe hat, plus whizzing through miles and miles of electric telephone wires have given her the zoomie-zoomies. She's not used to this! Just an ordinary do-nothing doll has become, and all because of me, a do-what? doll!"

Just how could he return a doll smitten with the zoomie-zoomies to Amy and to her family, who, unlike himself, were not accustomed to that curious magic? He was trapped in a delicate dilemma.

Tenderly he lifted Little Lydia out of his hat. Holding her tightly in his fist, he studied her with intense curiosity. He held her against his ear. He listened. Miniature rumblings of thunder were inside of her, thumping away, sounding like heartbeats, and even like do-re-mis! A musical doll. A do-nothing doll transformed into a musical doll! Boom! Boom! Boom! Just like the sound of the drum he could hear when he was working in the cellar of the Opera House, the practicing of the musicians above him on the stage.

What had he done? He realized he could not put Little Lydia back on her couch in her sand castle and surprise Amy in the morning as he had meant to do! He had to restore her to her old, perfect do-nothing condition, no questions asked.

Perhaps if he put her back in his hat, he could think better. First, he hid his magic bolt box back in its cubbyhole for his most out-of-the-way nuts and bolts. Then he put Little Lydia back in his stovepipe hat.

But up there her rumbles grew louder and louder and had begun to sound like words now, like a message in his own special bebop code.

"Little Lydia!" said Jimmy McGee. "Can you bebop a little louder? What did you say?"

"F-u-n!" came the bebop answer.

"Fun, eh?" repeated Jimmy McGee dubiously.

"Yes! F-u-n! F-u-n! F-u-n-n-y f-u-n!" came the answer as swiftly as a flash of lightning and in perfect bebop code.

"Well," said Jimmy McGee. "I'm glad you like it, but..."

He did not say what the "but" was. He didn't want to spoil Little Lydia's fun or hurt her feelings. She must have feelings now because she could talk in bebop words and make lightning-like zigzags.

Now, what a pickle Jimmy McGee was in! How could he change an electrified bebopping doll back into a real, right, regular do-nothing doll? How could he return Little Lydia to Amy in the curious condition she was in? A former do-nothing doll had now caught the zoomie-zoomies! She had become a rare doll who could give off zigzag shafts of lightning, speak bebop, and even go bang-bang on the lid of his splendid stovepipe hat, sounding like the musician who plays the timpani in the orchestra. She was a whole orchestra unto herself already.

You don't see that type of doll in any department store, a doll who can wham-bang on the timpani and probably so loudly that she'd shudder the opera house down with the applause!

For the first time ever, Jimmy McGee forgot to make his rounds!

7

Little Lydia and
the Zoomie-Zoomies

My, how the zoomie-zoomies had changed Little Lydia, and Jimmy McGee foresaw how this curious transformation was going to affect him and his life as a busy little plumber! He must do his best to keep this phenomenon under control!

Zoom! Zoom! Boom! Boom! Boom! Like thunder. Clang! Like a timpani! All going on, on top of him, in his stovepipe hat!

Naturally Jimmy McGee was worried. This banging showed that the magic might be catching. Not to him—he was in charge of his magic. All his rounds through the electric wires had kept his magic in perfect shape, so he would not do curious things unless he wanted to. But this was new to Little Lydia. Her strange behavior didn't bother him, not yet anyway. But, what about Amy? If she caught that magic?

Just suppose that he slipped Little Lydia back into her sand castle and laid her on her couch, as he had hoped to do. Amy would find her and joyously pick her up. Right away Amy might catch the magic and begin to do curious things. Bing! Bong! Boom!... on anything that was handy!

And suppose next she passed this magic on to her friend, Clarissa? Also to Mama and Papa? And what about the great dog Wags?

Imagine that beautiful dog catching the zoomie-zoomies. His growl already sounded like a deep, rising roll of thunder. Would he growl in bebop dog code? Sound like a bass drum? Would that dark brown-and-white wavy fur pop and sizzle and strike people with awe? If they tried to pet him, might they not catch the magic from him and begin to bark bebop or do other curious things themselves?

In fact, would all the people speak in bebop code, not only here around The Bizzy Bee, but also in the A & P even, the drugstore, sounding really curious? The Chamber of Commerce might advise people to stay away from that town! Poor Truro!

"Oh-oh-oh," groaned Jimmy McGee. "What have I wrought in my selfish search for thunder and lightning bolts? I have made Little Lydia an electrified bebopping doll. I must keep hold of her until I can cure her. Then she will speak in bebop no longer, no longer zigzag. Her hair will stop sizzling lightning. She will become a real, right do-nothing doll again, a Lydia, Little, doll, as entered in Amy's famous *Who's Who Book*!"

But the more Jimmy McGee worried, the louder Little Lydia bebopped and stomped around in his hat on top of his head!

"Fun! Fun! Funny fun!" she bebopped again.

"Funny. Yes, it is funny," said Jimmy McGee. In spite of his worries, Jimmy had to laugh. Who'd ever have thought this up? Have him in a pickle as curious as this?

Jimmy forgot that it was time for his next rounds! No pipes got banged that night, no shutters fastened securely, no drips in faucets stopped. Let the fish train come, let it go, lobsters and all. Jimmy McGee had sunk to the level of a do-nothing, not doll, plumber!

"Why," he asked himself, "did Little Lydia

have to come into my life?" He was sitting cross-legged, brooding, in the doorway of his summer headquarters. To make a hero of him, that's why.

It was in the book, the *Who's Who Book*, that he was a hero. Well, he *had* become a hero, right? He had rescued Little Lydia from Monstrous. Right? Wouldn't anybody think that was enough hero-making for one little plumber? Just as important as holding your finger in a hole in the dike and getting in one book after another? One book, Amy's, was enough for him!

But it was not in the book that he should, having rescued Little Lydia and become a hero, let her catch the zoomie-zoomies.

Maybe, he thought cautiously, just maybe, mind you, if Little Lydia were *out* of his hat, she'd stop that bebopping, those do-re-mis, that banging on a timpani! That's what she seemed to consider the carefully designed lid of his stovepipe hat to be.

"I'm in prison!" she bebopped now. *"In your stovepipe hat. In darkness some of the time. First, boom! Then zigzag light! Spooky. I can do these things now. Let me out. I'll show you, please!"*

Jimmy McGee replied, "In prison, yes, I can see that. Darkness, no! You, Little Lydia, you now have the zoomie-zoomies. That's magic. You can make little flashes of lightning. That's a great deal more than any ordinary people can do, including those dolls they sell that can do practically anything! Not what you can do, now. Still..."

"I'll share the magic! Please!"

Jimmy McGee was impressed with her pretty manners. Right or wrong, he made a decision. He would let her out of his hat, but not out of his headquarters. He must, sooner or later, get her back to Amy, grieving over having lost such an extraordinary doll. So he would let Little Lydia out of his hat, cure her, then get her back to Amy.

In six-sixty time, he wove a tough barrier of twigs and cranberry branches over the entrance-way to headquarters. Then he lifted Little Lydia out of his hat. What a relief! He scratched his head, and then he placed her in the darkest far-thermost recess of his headquarters. Enchanted, he watched her zigzag flashes come and go.

She was like a lightning bug, twinkling here and there back in the cave. Now he saw her, now he didn't. In one of those moments when he didn't see her, Lydia, Little, alighted on the lid of his little strong box. She had already discovered where he had hidden that box. Little Lydia's magic was recharged.

Jimmy McGee did not know this. He'd been watching her flashes come and go. What he hoped was they would stay gone and that by letting her out of his hat, her magic would wear thin.

Alas! Nothing of what he had hoped by releasing her from her hat prison happened. Instead, her zigzag flashes became more and more frequent.

Again he forgot his rounds. He just couldn't take his eyes off Little Lydia. She mesmerized him. Night passed that way. In the morning he neglected to bang the pipes anyplace. The days were getting shorter, the nights longer and cooler. He still had the sense not to leave Little Lydia alone in his headquarters, not even to check on The Bizzy Bee.

However, he did watch the goings and the comings of Amy and Clarissa, who might be looking for shells or anything to add to the beauty of their castle and its town, or to go paddling.

In the evening, late, a young person out strolling said, "Have you ever seen so many fireflies as there are this year? There must be a nesting place for them up there at the dune. Their lights come on, their lights go off."

"M-m-m," agreed her companion, and on they walked arm in arm down the beach enjoying these last evenings of summer.

So far, nothing bad had happened because of Jimmy McGee's neglect of his people. Some complained a little that the hot water hadn't been coming on on the dot as it usually did and that they had slept later than usual. They did not get down to the beach until practically lunchtime, still yawning and stretching from too much sleep.

Jimmy McGee let his work slip more and more. He never made his rounds. People in The Bizzy Bee wondered. Papa said, "I hope we won't have to get a plumber. Seems to me things are going to pot!" It was now getting toward the end of August. Many people had already left Cape Cod to get their children ready for school, buy sneakers and pencils and erasers.

They had left without Jimmy McGee's even having reminded them to turn off the water at the taps in the cellar and empty out all the tanks so that the pipes wouldn't freeze and burst come winter. Also to bolt down the shutters. Amy and her family were still here. Once he heard Amy say, "There's still a chance Little Lydia will wash ashore. Miracles do happen!"

And every day they carefully scanned the water's edge hoping that by some miracle they would find their lost Little Lydia. Guilt, though not very deep, sometimes swept over Jimmy McGee.

Once in a while he reminded himself, "Remember the hurricane, Jimmy McGee. Lobelia! Coming soon, you know." Amy and her family must be ready for a speedy departure if his predictions were right. Predictions? He hadn't kept track of anything. He pulled himself up short. "Oh, but they can count on me, Jimmy McGee!"

But he seemed to not really care. He wanted to spend all his time watching Little Lydia. It was as though he were under a spell. And was she ever worth watching! With every passing hour her zigzags flashed more brightly. Her blue eyes, always so very blue, now cast off magical beams, and when she fastened them on him, they sent off tiny sparks.

He realized that she had discovered where he had hidden his precious magic bolt box. But instead of hiding it in a still more secret place, he let her alight on it, just to see what would happen next. He wasn't going to open it. Oh no! He still had that much sense. He'd open it when the right time came. But he rather liked the very faint rumble of thunder in there and what he imagined the little streaks of lightning were like.

Whenever he lifted Little Lydia off this magic bolt box, he realized that she had received a powerful charge! One time he saw her walking, not on her own two legs that were not geared for walking anyway, but on what looked like shimmering stilts. They were like miniature streaks of lightning and were bright gold. Very pretty. Sometimes she jumped up and down and hopped about as though she were on crooked pogo sticks.

She should be in a circus, thought Jimmy McGee admiringly.

Sometimes she seemed to be suspended halfway between the dry grassy floor of his headquarters and the ceiling with its straggly, lacy roots. Her tousled yellow hair would get tangled in the grass roots until they, too, became charged and lighted up the place like a smart cafe.

Then when that curious exhibition was over, she made her descent to Jimmy McGee's bolt box and fastened her eloquent blue eyes on him. This made him uneasy.

No wonder his work suffered. Then it oc-

curred to him that he might have a rival! Little
Lydia was beginning to do the things that he
did! She looked at his nuts and bolts, saw one
in the wrong place, polished it a little on her
calico dress so it shone, and put it in the right
place. She looked at his pipes and fastened her
eyes especially on the scrolls. She might tamper
with these treasures, especially the one with the
Who's Who Book where his name was and hers.

Perhaps she would take off and zoomie-zoomie
through the wires the way he did, but on her
own, not in his bombazine bag or his stovepipe

hat! She might begin to think *she* was boss of the bolts, that no longer was she, Little Lydia, a do-nothing doll, but was now a doll girl plumber. Perhaps she would bang the pipes and make the houses shudder wherever happenstance might make her. Wake the people up in the middle of the night even! Hide under the bedclothes...

And o-o-ops! Worst thing of all! She might somehow figure out how to unlatch his magic bolt box and set those valuable specimens free!

He must watch her very closely. She might zoomie-zoomie away and never come back, doing shenanigans all on her own! *He* was the *hero. He* was the one who had rescued her from Monstrous! Was that gratitude on her part?

But none of these thoughts irritated Jimmy McGee for very long. He was under an ever-deepening spell watching and listening to Little Lydia!

Once she bebopped, *"Now I jump over the candlestick!"* and the whole place lighted up. Of course there wasn't any *candlestick*!

Jimmy McGee had to laugh, and he clapped his hands. She must have learned that line from listening to Amy reading Mother Goose to Clarissa.

Now and then, from habit, he scanned his storm book ledger. He was reminded then that Hurricane Lobelia was soon coming, or not coming. He had not bothered to check her course, not bothered to figure whether it was coming, today, tomorrow, next week, and where? Or ever?

He didn't care. Let hurricanes come. Let hurricanes go. But let him laze and ponder the phenomenon of Little Lydia, the bebop doll, caught up in curious magic.

Sometimes, bemused, Jimmy McGee wondered what he used to do before he had rescued Little Lydia from the wave named Monstrous and become a hero.

He now slept more than the two-three secs he used to allow himself. But one evening he was awakened as by a bolt! He was shaken out of his sloth by an ominous signal from Little Lydia herself!

Wide awake now and sitting in his doorway— at least he still had the sense to always do that— he was prepared to see and *did* see Little Lydia poised on one of her zigzag stilt walks, poised as though to go somewhere. She bebopped, *"Wake up, lazy McGee! You have missed the Cape Codder. The fish and lobster may spoil! Then what will people in the Copley Plaza do? I'm off,"* and bebopping again her favorite threat, *"Now I jump over the candlestick!"* she did jump over Jimmy McGee's head and was out to see the world, catch up with the fish train, and not let lobsters spoil!

But Jimmy McGee grabbed her by her sparkling frizzy hair in the nick of time! For all he knew, she might by now be able to zoomie-zoomie even faster than he, and then he'd never catch her!

But he had her! He popped her in his stove-pipe hat along with his thunder and lightning bolt box, which he had the sense to retrieve, and he clamped the hat tightly on his head.

Little Lydia could not get out. After a few sharp bing-bangs up there, zigzag, petulant stomping, she subsided and lay low.

That attack of the zoomie-zoomies had worn itself out. Jimmy McGee wished that would be the end forever. But he knew she would re-charge herself on account of sharing company with the little strong box holding the tiny thunder and lightning bolts, tiny bolts to be sure, but large enough for Little Lydia—or for anybody.

Suddenly, like a streak of lightning, there came the bebop words from the stovepipe hat, *"Get to work, lazy Jimmy McGee!"*

"Can't you just bebop, *'Fun, funny fun?'*" pleaded Jimmy McGee. He was affronted. A busy, busy pipe-and-bong plumber man being talked to in this rude way! Where were those pretty manners of hers?

"No!" bebopped Little Lydia. *"Or, I will have to do your work for you!"*

All this bebop conversation was accompanied by the zigzag hopping around upstairs in his hat, not at all comfortable. But the effect on Jimmy McGee was electric! While trying to gather his wits, there came the next bebop.

"Remember the hurricane, Lobelia, lazy Mr. McGee! Get to work!"

"Yes. No," said Jimmy McGee. No one had ever before spoken to him, much less given him orders. As far as he knew, only one special person, Amy, who had listed him in her book, even knew about him at all. Even the great dog Wags didn't sniff around the cellar for him. He was a private man, a little fellow, a plumber, a hero!

"You're right," he said.

He put his best banging pipes in his bombazine bag along with other special nuts and bolts needed for hurricane work. He slung it over his shoulder like a soldier. As though electrified, he got back into being the real, right Jimmy McGee again.

He swung into action with Little Lydia and his important bolt box stashed safely away in his stovepipe hat. Up top all was quiet right now...

Jimmy McGee, grateful for the silence, had a few moments to study his notes and the quotes in his pipes concerning hurricanes, past, present, and future. The one that concerned him now was, of course, Lobelia. According to his calculations, she might be coming this way any day now, very soon!

But Little Lydia couldn't keep still for very long. She did not like being back in captivity in the stovepipe hat! She began to hop around again and to make a terrible clatter not only on its tin top lid, but also on the strong little box with the thunder and lightning bolts.

"Let me out!" Little Lydia bebopped.

"No!" said Jimmy McGee. "You have to stay up there, and please be quiet! I'm thinking. You take my mind off my work with your curious hops, skips, and jumps. You know—you learned it from me—that there is going to be a hurricane, coming any time soon. And hurricanes, whatever their names, mean *work* for me. You get yourself back to being a regular do-nothing, say-nothing doll again. Then you can be free and go home and be Amy's Little Lydia again. Practice!" he urged her.

All the answer he got to this eloquent plea was the same old message, *"Let me out!"*

But Jimmy McGee just clamped his hat down even more firmly so that it would be impossible for her to escape and expose the population to the zoomie-zoomies. He hoped that she had not made a dent in his elegant and famous hat, which he had worn on so many strange and curious adventures, all written up in his scrolls.

So now, really to test his own recovery from the many days of sloth, but also to see how Little Lydia would react to being out of headquarters, he zoomie-zoomied to The Bizzy Bee, checked the cellar and the faucets, but did not bang them hard, for they had all gone to bed, everyone there in the cottage.

In bed, Clarissa was whispering to Amy. "Amy," she said. "Has it strucken you that there haven't been as many bang-bangs on the pipes as there used to be?"

"Of course," said Amy. "Just means Jimmy McGee is off on one of his strange and curious adventures. Nighty-night."

Jimmy McGee overheard this bedtime talk. Strange and curious it had been all right; and all had happened just a few feet away from The Bizzy Bee.

In the cellar he gave just the faintest little tap on one of the pipes, a good-night tap, and he and Little Lydia returned to headquarters.

Little Lydia had been remarkably quiet.

8

Good-by, Good-by
to Summer Headquarters

After this short trial excursion to The Bizzy Bee with Little Lydia in his hat, Jimmy McGee bebopped up to Little Lydia, "You are a heroine! You'll be in a library maybe some day, in one of my scrolls anyway. You waked me up. Thank you!"

"You're welcome!" she bebopped.

"We're partners," said Jimmy McGee. "The hero-heroine partnership!"

"No!" Lydia, Little, bebopped vehemently. *"Not as long as I'm trapped in your stovepipe hat! I don't like the smell of stove polish!"*

"Too bad!" said Jimmy. "But I can't let you out. You might get lost again. Another

Monstrous might grab you. Make the best of it. We're going on my rounds. You used to say, *'Fun!'*"

"Fun!" bebopped Lydia faintly, almost like a whisper, an echo.

Hesitantly, Jimmy McGee thought, "Well, maybe her magic is wearing thin?" So he hoped anyway and went off in six-sixty time to do the work he loved ... whamming pipes here, whamming pipes there. He didn't even stop to take one of his short one-two secs' rests.

Very early the next morning he zoomied over to The Bizzy Bee cottage. Making up for lost time, did he ever wham-bang the pipes there! He waked everybody up much earlier than usual because ... look at the clouds!

The sky was dark, brooding, menacing. All was quiet. "The calm before a storm," thought Jimmy McGee. A great storm was coming—Lobelia! He whisked off on his rounds up and down Cape Cod, the north side, the south side, the end up to Provincetown; and he saw to the dogs, the cats, the train ... choo-choo-choo ... banging all pipes where necessary, tightening a bolt here, looking at switches there ... everything in his usual line of business. He was the real, right Jimmy McGee again...no longer that strange, slothful do-nothing Jimmy McGee.

His do-nothing days were over! You have to thank Little Lydia for that. First she had enchanted him with her own case of the zoomie-zoomies. But then she had roused him, saved him, restored him to his true self...Jimmy McGee, a plumber, a banger on pipes! Now people would know about the storm. Hurricane Lobelia might or might not come this way. Hurricanes can be capricious! But at any rate, he had sounded the alert!

His rounds took him far, far away, even to the little church near Ipswich, where he had captured his rare bolts, safely stored in the tight little box still, and he sped even way, way down to Maine and all the little islands off the coast. Here he was warning everybody about Lobelia with his bangs on shutters and pipes, his ringing of church bells and fire alarms, helping them to close up and get their boats moored, to batten down the hatches, to go away from home, if home were near the sea, and to take refuge inland. He thought of everything, and his magic was so strong that people got the message and did what was expected.

"Close up! Close up! Go home!" many said, and frantically made preparations.

The wind was rising now. At The Bizzy Bee, Amy's mother said, "My! Look at the sky...so gray! Hear the shutters banging? And we had only just latched them!

"Maybe it is a hurricane. I haven't listened to the radio or read the *Boston Globe,* have you?" she asked some neighbors.

Most people had not. They were too busy having last clambakes and cookouts, farewell-to-summer get-togethers, picnics. "See you same time next summer," all that sort of happy, yet sad goings-on. Summer gone, hard work, a long winter ahead...

"If it *is* a hurricane, what's the name of this one?" someone asked. "Lobelia!" someone else replied.

"Is the eye of it going to be here in North Truro on Cape Cod?" an indignant, elegant elderly man asked. He consulted his fine gold watch as though that might tell him. And he waved his handsome cane in the air, back and forth, as if to blow the storm away...rid Cape Cod of it.

"Maybe we should leave a day earlier than we had planned," suggested Papa. "After all, school starts in just a few days anyhow."

Mama agreed. They'd all rather be back at home on Garden Lane in Washington, D.C., than here in a hurricane.

"Something told me we should get ourselves ready to leave ahead of time this summer," said Mama, "so I have already packed most of our things. We should be able to finish up quickly."

"Everyone be ready by seven o'clock," said Papa.

Amy and Clarissa had already been having fun packing, unpacking, and repacking their little suitcases and the carton of toys and books. They now hurried off to pack the shells, some big, some little, that they had collected during the summer.

Many of their neighbors decided to leave, too, and scurried around here and there. "Don't forget this, don't forget that!"

"I loaned Frank Gunther my binoculars. Did he bring them back?" someone asked his wife.

"Don't know. Don't know," she answered.

All this activity was thanks to the doings of Jimmy McGee, a banger on pipes, a little fellow, a plumber...a *hero*!

He was happy to see and to hear the activity in the cottages. He'd just gotten back from his rounds, Bar Harbor, everywhere, and he, too, was impatient to be off to his winter headquarters in Mount Rose Park behind a little waterfall tumbling into a sparkling brook with violets on its banks.

Then he would unpack his bombazine bag, lay aside his summer banging pipes, and replace them with sturdier wintertime pipes and tools. He wanted to get over to Amy's house on Garden Lane before Amy and her family and Clarissa and Wags arrived there in the old gray Dodge. Get the whole house in apple-pie order for them!

He intended that Little Lydia, who had been singularly quiet while all this hustle and bustle was going on, would be there at number 3017 when Amy would open the front door and say, "Hello, house!" And what a joyous surprise she would have if it all worked out as he hoped!

But he was ahead of himself. Still here in

Truro, he banged the pipes once again to remind people about faucets, to empty out all the water so the pipes wouldn't freeze and burst, to roll up the hose, to turn off the taps in the cellars and the faucets upstairs.

He felt exultant. He was back to work again and with no more orders from Little Lydia, the bebop doll. Now *he* was the boss! In some houses where lazy, slowpoke types of people lived, he banged the pipes so hard that the owners thought they were bursting and yelled for the plumber, who couldn't be everywhere at once. So he took the phone off the hook and went back to bed with liniment on his legs.

By now Jimmy had checked all his charts and had his bearings. He knew the eye of the storm would not be here in Truro. Though it might veer out to sea and wear itself out, the edge of the storm would be bad anyway. He was glad he had slam-banged the pipes as hard as he had.

He did know, though, that the storm would be worse in Washington, D.C., and he wanted to be back home in his winter headquarters before the storm broke there and to have Amy's family get home before then, too.

The waters of the Potomac might be so high

they might whish right over the feet of the great, beautiful statue of Abraham Lincoln... who knows? The accuracy of Jimmy McGee's forecasting had been more than a little bit dimmed by the magic spell he had been under while watching the curious antics of Little Lydia. A certain foreboding about Little Lydia did persist now and then, but he shrugged it off.

His rounds completed, Jimmy McGee zoomied back to The Bizzy Bee, and from the cellar window he surveyed the going-away preparations. He was happy to see that Papa had backed the old gray Dodge to the kitchen door. The back was open and all the car doors, too. Everyone was busy putting luggage inside somewhere, wherever there was room. Amy was clutching her *Who's Who Book* in her hand like a person taking inventory and making sure everything and everybody was accounted for.

"We never did find Little Lydia," she said sadly.

"Never," echoed Clarissa.

Neither of them realized that she was not far away hopping around in the stovepipe hat of Jimmy McGee. How he wished he could just pop her into the box of dolls and toys when no one was looking! But a zigzag sound on top of his head made him realize he couldn't do that.

Amy looked down sadly at her box of dolls. "I thought Little Lydia just might have shown up, just might have. Because," she said, "it says in my book, 'But I hope she will be rescued by a *hero*!' Well, she never did come back. But, anyway, I still have her little blue shawl." And she put it on top of her *Who's Who Book.*

"Woe! Woe!" said Clarissa. This was a word she had lately read in some sad story and now used whether or not it fitted the case.

No one needed to worry about Wags, the great and beautiful springer spaniel. He had been ready for a long time. He'd been sitting in the driver's seat from the moment Papa had backed the car to the kitchen door. Everyone knew he would not leave this driver's seat, not even to chase the Cape Codder up the tracks, until Papa got in and made him move over. Wags would then sit beside him so that Papa could take hold of the steering wheel.

Everybody stood still a moment to look at and laugh at Wags. Right now he still had his left front leg on the armrest of the car door. He looked like a driver in disguise...a dog chauffeur. His red drinking bowl was on the floor by the clutch. There was a bottle of water beside it, so Wags knew the ride was going to be a long one. That made him happy, and he moved Papa's old gray sock from side to side in his mouth.

This sock looked ridiculous, but he always carried it around with him unless he was eating or drinking. Once in a while Mama had to wash it, but she had the mate to it, a substitute, which Papa had to wear a day or two first to get his smell on it. Wags was a comical sight; but the family did not have time to take a snapshot. Too bad!

Papa said, "Everybody ready? If there's going to be a hurricane, we want to be home before it gets there."

Mama said, "I'm ready. Leftover food is in my box here, fruit juice in the thermos, I have my purse. This is the quickest closing-up we ever made. Oh, wait!" she said. "I left Wagsie's spare sock on the porch to dry. I'll get it." This she did and dropped it in Amy's carton in the back, the last carton to be put in the car.

Papa was in the back, making sure that everything was stashed in securely and that the tailgate would close. Jimmy McGee zoomied to the front of the car and tightened some nuts and bolts under the hood. He banged the engine lightly. He knew it was in fine shape. Then he sped off to the kitchen to watch the leave-taking. Perhaps Little Lydia could watch it, too, with those electric blue eyes of hers that might enable her to see through stovepipe hats!

Then Papa slammed the tailgate, which did just barely close, and locked it up.

"Move over, Wags," Papa said. Wags did move over a little, and Papa got in the driver's seat. Wags dropped his sock for a minute and licked Papa's cheek to show how much he loved him. Then he put his sock back in his mouth. Papa started the car to let it warm up.

"Well!" Papa exclaimed. "What do you know! I don't know what magic touch I have suddenly developed, but it started. We won't have to stop at the garage to check it. This car has a soul of its own! It fixes itself!"

Mama got in and sat in the front seat beside Wags, who was happy to be made to sit closer to Papa again. Amy and Clarissa were already in the back seat, where they kneeled and cupped their chins in their hands and looked out the back window. Amy stood Bear between them so he could see out, too.

"Let's see who can see The Bizzy Bee the longest when we get going," said Clarissa.

"I bet Bear will," said Amy. She propped him up so his chin just barely rested on the top of the upholstery. "There!" she said. "See what you can, Bear. See Jimmy McGee if you can!"

She and Clarissa laughed. "The banger-on-the pipes man!" Amy explained to Bear.

"All right, then," said Papa. "We're off!"

"Zoomie-zoomie-zoomie," said Amy, laughing.

"Zoomie-zoomie-zoomie on the zoomie-zoomie trail," sang Clarissa.

Papa started up slowly.

"Good-by, good-by to everything," sang Amy and Clarissa. "Good-by, summer!" They felt a little sad.

They watched the little cottage where they had spent a whole summer grow smaller and smaller, dwindle away. It looked cold and forlorn already, a not-lived-in house, tiny and fragile on the top of the dune. No one in it to wake up to the sound of Jimmy McGee's banging on the pipes. Then, after a bend in the road, they couldn't see it any more.

No one could say who had seen it the longest; all had seen it the longest.

"Maybe Bear saw it the longest," Amy said. "Did you, Bear?"

Amy took Bear in her arms and hugged him. "Bear did," she said. "I think he did."

They couldn't know that Jimmy McGee was watching the old gray Dodge growing smaller and smaller and gathering speed now down the hard, sandy road, sending flecks of sand and gravel behind it and a little puff of smoke.

Nor could they know that Jimmy McGee would be at their home on Garden Lane in Washington, banging the pipes there to greet them when they arrived and to make their house ready for living in again.

During the leave-taking, Little Lydia had been remarkably quiet. Now suddenly she be-bopped, *"Fun!"*

Jimmy McGee's apprehensions were realized. She was not yet restored to being a do-nothing doll! Well, perhaps she was like Wags and anticipated a trip to somewhere, like the great thunder-and-lightning-bolt excursion, or perhaps some new and curious adventure Jimmy McGee had in mind?

Jimmy McGee swiftly made his final check around The Bizzy Bee. Everything was fine... windows boarded up, doors locked, only a few final drops of water falling from the outside garden faucet, and they would soon stop. A thin little cat from down the road came walking as though bowlegged. She sat under the faucet and watched the drops fall, licking one once in a while, batting another with her paw.

Then Jimmy McGee zoomied over to his headquarters to close it up for the winter. Not hard at all. All he did was shove his summer banging pipes way, way back in the cave, fold up his bombazine hammock, and lay it neatly on his scrolls, his summer scroll library. He pushed them into the farthermost recess. They were his most valued items, his research library.

He left the entranceway the way it always was in case, in a bad storm, a blizzard perhaps, a scared little field mouse or rabbit, even a hermit crab, might want to get in and be safe...be refugees!

Then Jimmy McGee made sure his hat was clamped down securely on his head. Inside was his special box with its thunder and lightning bolts and Little Lydia, who was buzzing around up there.

He had a plan. He aimed to surprise Amy when she began to unpack. She would discover in her box her Little Lydia, no longer her lost best-loved doll. Amy would be puzzled, of course, but imagine her joy! First, of course, he had to make sure Little Lydia no longer had the zoomie-zoomies.

Now then, he was ready to zoom down the wires to his home, his winter headquarters. How the winds hummed as he whizzed along! They sounded like the strumming on some strange stringed instrument.

Suddenly Little Lydia, recharged from this lightning-like journey through the wires, hopped up and down in Jimmy McGee's stovepipe hat and bebopped, *"Fun! Funny fun!"*

Like Wags, she was happy to be on the move again, even though she was locked up in a stovepipe hat and could not enjoy the view!

"Oh, dear!" groaned Jimmy McGee.

By the time she had finished a few more of these happy bebop messages, which she had turned into a quite pleasant little song, Jimmy

McGee had zoomied into Mount Rose Park in Washington, D.C.

Probably, back in Truro, Amy and her family had only just turned around the bend of the road. And Bear was looking out the window!

9

Jimmy McGee in His Winter Headquarters

Home now, Jimmy McGee put thoughts of summertime behind him. He waited a moment longer behind the little waterfall at the entrance to his winter headquarters. He liked the way it smelled here, of moss and dampness and rocks. The little waterfall was like a silvery curtain between him and the world outside. He liked the sound of it splashing gently into the little brook below. On a sunny day all was sparkly, like little diamonds. And when the sun set, the streams of water took on the look of sparklers on the Fourth of July.

It was good to be back. Violets lined the banks of the little brook. They were still in blossom. He stepped inside. His winter headquarters were under a little knoll. In the wintertime children went sledding down the knoll, through the tree-lined path to where the little brook joined a larger one.

His headquarters had smooth earth-colored boulders. There were crevices between them for his pipes and scrolls and things. The boulders were wonderful, all of a different shape, some flat at the bottom, some rounded, and he used them for many purposes. Some went to the top of the cave like steps, and one was like the stone throne of an ancient king, its surface rounded and comfortable.

Jimmy McGee always sat on his throne to bring his scrolls up to date or to polish his nuts and bolts. Also in the cave were tough roots of trees winding here and there, good for gymnastics. People taking a stroll overhead would never believe a place of such magic existed right under their very feet. The moss was thick up there, and also a creeping kind of flower called periwinkle.

But now to work! Jimmy McGee slung his bombazine bag on a sturdy root near his throne. He kept his stovepipe hat clamped firmly on his head.

The old gray Dodge could not travel with the six-sixty speed that he could! Probably it would not arrive until late afternoon.

Anybody could tell that there was a storm coming. Winds were rising, and the sky was ominous! Just so Amy and her family arrived before the big storm struck! But to Jimmy McGee, the expert predictor, it seemed that it would hold off until late in the day, and the old gray Dodge would make it by then.

First he tidied up his headquarters. Evidently there had been curious little animals in here now and then . . . rabbits mainly, he thought. He made sure all his fine nuts and bolts and pipes were in their proper nooks, all labeled, as always.

But somehow he had the feeling that his headquarters were not exactly right. He sensed that something might be awry! He checked through it swiftly but saw nothing unusual. At the same time he was looking for the best place for Little Lydia to stay while he did his necessary work preparing for a storm. Some of it might take him over telephone wires, some already shaking in the wind, but they were the last things he wanted Little Lydia to be close to...get herself further recharged!

He decided to lay her on a nice flat boulder, high up in his headquarters. Slightly above her, there was another large boulder, a sort of ledge. Suppose a little field mouse or a squirrel, looking for nuts, came in and sat on that flat ledge. Lydia, Little, would have something to look at, and it could look at her!

Just as he was about to take this important step, she stomped around up there in his stovepipe hat, making his head itch! Didn't she realize that now she was in a big city with presidents and congresses and monuments and music...not in sunny little old Truro by the sea?

"You let me out, McGee, or I'll sizzle and frizzle your hair!" Little Lydia bebopped.

"All right, Little Lydia," Jimmy McGee answered. "All right. That's just what I'm going to do. Be calm. Don't bebop. Be good. Be a do-nothing doll! We're home now, in my elegant winter headquarters."

"I can't see through stovepipe hats!" came the bebop answer.

"Of course not," said Jimmy McGee. "Soon, very soon, you're going back to Amy. You will see her and Clarissa and Bear, all your old friends, Wags and Mama and Papa. But first you must get over the zoomie-zoomies. Away from all the zigzag journeys we have taken, you will be cured."

"I'm not sick! Let me out!" Little Lydia demanded.

"Sh-sh-sh!" said Jimmy McGee. "Don't shout! I've found the right spot for you, in my winter palace, not as elegant as your sand castle, but comfortable, very high up, from which you will have a fine view of what goes on, if anything. So, here we are!" he said.

Then Jimmy McGee took off his stovepipe hat with a grand flourish, bowed, and said, "You are out of my stovepipe hat now."

He laid her gently on the flat rock, where a sort of plush-like green moss made a pretty couch for her. "There's a ledge a little above you to your left in case some visitor might come. Stay right there! Don't think you can go zooming around any more or back into my hat, what you call 'prison,' you will go!"

"Thank you!" she bebopped.

Although Jimmy McGee preferred that she would have said nothing, he was again impressed by her pretty manners. And how lovely she looked with her electric blue eyes, which she fastened immediately on the ledge just a little to the left and not far above her!

He assured himself that this was the sensible thing to do. If the storm became as mighty as predicted, no matter how tightly he clung to his hat, somehow the wind might whip it off. Then, off Little Lydia would blow, and what would happen to her next? A challenge even harder than rescuing her from Monstrous! One rescue was enough.

But the most important thing of all was that in her own lofty domain she was far away from his strong box with the thunder and lightning bolts. He put the box on a boulder and began to sweep out his headquarters.

Still, he was worried. "Sound of the waterfall pretty?" he asked.

Little Lydia did not answer.

"Do the nuts and bolts all around you make you feel like you're back in Truro?" Jimmy McGee asked.

Still Little Lydia did not answer. She just lay

there, looking at the other boulder near her, just above her, like a shelf, the way she used to stare at the ceiling of his headquarters in North Truro just after the rescue and before she caught the zoomie-zoomies. She was like a doll in an exhibition.

Jimmy McGee put his thunder and lightning bolt box back into his hat and clamped it on his head. But now there was no Little Lydia in it. He was reluctant to leave, but he had to. He had to get to Garden Lane before the family arrived.

"Well, bye!" said Jimmy McGee. "I'll be back soon. And soon, if you keep on improving, back to Amy you shall go!"

Little Lydia did not bebop. "That's very good," thought Jimmy McGee. "She really is making tremendous progress toward getting back to being a do-nothing doll."

He looked at her tenderly. All she was doing was staring with those electric blue eyes straight up at the boulder, shelf-like, just a little above hers. Staring at what? Or at nothing? "She can't move her eyes, so she has to stare somewhere," he reasoned.

Jimmy McGee then was ready to go. He slung

his bombazine bag with his most needed hurricane work tools in it over his shoulder, and off he zoomied.

He was still uneasy about leaving Little Lydia alone. Curious how those electric blue eyes of hers seemed to light up the semi-twilight look the cave always had! But it couldn't be helped. He had to leave her and go about his hurricane business.

He did a great deal of regular Jimmy McGee plumber work here and there. Then he sped over to number 3017 Garden Lane, where, right now, the old gray Dodge, headlights on, was slowly rounding the corner and heading for home. It had just barely beat the hurricane home, for now, as Papa parked the car in front of the pretty three-story red-brick house, the fury of the storm broke. Wind snatched the orange fruit off the ginkgo trees and sent them flying through the air like Ping-Pong balls.

"Don't step on the ginkgoes!" screamed Amy. "They smell awful!"

"Don't mind that!" screamed Mama. "Everybody get into the house as fast as you can! Branches might fall on you or trees topple over!"

Mama frantically unlocked the front door. Wags was the first one in, tripping everybody up as they staggered in with cartons, suitcases, and boxes. He was so glad to be home that he raced back and forth all over the house and then back to the front door, counting them all. Jimmy McGee watched all this from the cellar window, where he was already at work.

The family set the cartons and suitcases down wherever they could, many of them in the kitchen. Wags sniffed each one of them, wagged his tail when he saw his red bowl, and dropped Papa's soggy old sock in it. This meant he was hungry...and thirsty! Then he picked his sock up again and tore around the house with it dangling from his mouth and looking absurd.

But no one had time to laugh. And they did— just in time—get everything in!

Down below in the cellar, Jimmy McGee thought, "The way they're tearing around up there, you'd think they all had the zoomie-zoomies and without benefit of Little Lydia."

Now the rains came down, tearing in a horizontal streak up Garden Lane, going in the direction of Mount Rose Park, up the hill.

"Look at that rain!" exclaimed Amy at the

front window. "It's tearing by in one straight sheet."

"It's traveling," said Clarissa. "It's not coming down!"

"Don't you believe it isn't coming down, too," said Papa. "Look at the street. Gushing rivers in the gutters, rushing down toward the Potomac!"

But everybody and everything was in, in their pretty, strongly built house. Clarissa's house, painted a pale pink, was just a few doors away, but her family had not returned yet from their important travels. She was going to stay with Amy until they did get back.

"Everybody here," said Amy happily. "Everybody except Little Lydia!"

"Maybe we'll see her go rushing by in the gutter river!" said Clarissa.

Little did anyone know how very near Little Lydia really was...just up the hill in Jimmy McGee's winter headquarters.

But now Jimmy McGee slam-banged the pipes in the cellar. He, too, had Little Lydia on his mind and wanted to get back to her. He made the house reverberate like the strings of a giant and explosive bass violin! This was Jimmy

McGee's way of giving the family a rousing welcome.

Then he paused for a moment and listened to the homecoming upstairs. At first they could not tear themselves from the windows. But then they began to drag suitcases and cartons from the kitchen all over the house so Mama would have room to work. They were all hungry.

Papa lugged one carton down to the cellar. "Hey!" said Amy. "Those are my things, not cellar things!"

"I'll bring it up later," said Papa, panting. "Right now we need the space in the kitchen. My back aches. I'll turn on the water while I'm down here." He hummed and sang a little old-time song to remind himself how you do this. " 'On at the bong, then on with the faucets! And then we have water!' " The "bong" in the cellar was the main cutoff of water for a whole house.

In his corner Jimmy McGee nodded his head in appreciation. He could have done this for them, but he didn't want to deprive Papa of the joys of doing cellar work.

Meanwhile, Mama was preparing snacks from the food they'd brought back from Cape Cod. "Ouch! My back!" she said. "Wags! You just plain take up too much space in the front seat. You don't give me enough room..."

Wags, dejected, slunked behind the dining room door for a moment. Then he backed out with his limp old sock dangling out of his mouth when Mama said, "There, there, Wagsie. I didn't mean to hurt your feelings. Good old Wagsie boy!"

Heartened by these words, Wags backed all the way out and tore all over the house...up the stairs to the third floor, then slid the two flights back down on his belly, and then raced through the living room and the dining room, bunching up the rugs, and then to the kitchen, where he pawed Mama's skirts and pushed his red bowl all over the floor, panting and imploring Mama for water!

Jimmy McGee, down in the cellar, tightening some loose bolts here and there, was enjoying the upstairs sounds. "That dog Wags is practically a zoomie-zoomie dog already," he thought. "Imagine the whole population of this house with the zoomie-zoomies, speaking in bebop and walking on zigzag streaks of lightning!"

The thought was staggering! Luckily Little Lydia was safe and sound in his winter headquarters, where she was contaminating no one. If she were still in his stovepipe hat, she would perhaps be bebopping, *"Fun! Fun! Funny fun!"*

He wished she were up there in his hat enjoying with him the homecoming! He missed her. He would really be sorry when the right and proper time came for them to part.

Now Papa came up from the cellar, having turned on the tap so Mama could get water from the kitchen faucet. At the same time Jimmy McGee gave a big rousing slam-bang on the water pipes, a welcoming bang, and the water spurted out...bang-spurt-spuff! "Like Old Faithful in Yellowstone!" said Papa, and everybody laughingly said, "Let's all have a glass of Old Faithful!"

"Old Washington, D.C., water is good enough for me," said Papa. He eyed the water pouring out in a steady stream now. "Have to let it run a bit," he said. "Been shut off all summer."

"O-o-oh..." Everybody groaned. All had glasses in outstretched hands for some D.C. water to quench their thirst.

"Phew!" said Papa. "I'm thirsty! Whatever was in that last carton I lugged downstairs? Weighed a ton of bricks!"

"Books are not bricks," said Amy. "That carton has my books, my dolls—all but one of them anyway..."

Jimmy McGee had already seen what was in that last heavy carton that Papa was talking about. And what he had seen, tucked in at the last moment in Truro, was the *Who's Who Book* by Amy. This box was to be Little Lydia's final destination, and the final end to all the perplexing hero business. From then on, bang-bang, zoomie-zoomie, back to his real, right regular jobs—being just a plumber, a little fellow, a banger on pipes. Mission of having to become a hero accomplished...well, almost accomplished...for a second time.

For a moment longer, Jimmy McGee listened to the sounds upstairs in the kitchen. What a happy life Little Lydia, the do-nothing doll, had here! Much better kind of life than going on the zoomie-zoomies with him all the time, stashed away in his stovepipe hat. Ah, now, soon he'd see if her recovery had really been complete.

Upstairs everybody was drinking water now. "Ugh!" said Amy, and spit her mouthful into the sink.

"You'll get used to it again," said Mama.

Clarissa didn't care what the water tasted like and drank two full glassfuls almost without stopping. Papa, too. "D.C. water, not Old Faithful," he said. And Wags. How he drank! He slurped down his whole bowlful of water without taking a breath. Most seemed to go on the floor. People stood back while he then shook his head and his whole body as though he had been in for a splendid swim.

"He drinks like a horse," marveled Amy. "He wants some more."

All of them stopped short in what they were doing to watch Wags drink and to hear him! It was a spectacular sight and almost made the water they were drinking taste really good. Anyway it *was* wet. Then they went on with fixing the picnic supper.

Jimmy McGee decided that it was time to get on with his hurricane work, which he did in six-sixty time, because he so desperately wanted to get back to headquarters and make certain Little Lydia was safe and sound there, staring, staring with her electric blue eyes at the rock near her...

He zoomie-zoomied off in the wind and the rain and the crackling sound of branches being

torn from the trees. He checked everything...
cellars, bridges, parks, trollies, seeing what
wires were down. He even went to Echo Park
to make certain the carousel had been boarded
up and the flying horses made safe. Then he
banged the cellars where he found those people
who were not doing what they were supposed to
be doing, but were carousing, partying, saying,
"Ho-ho! What's a little old hurricane anyway?"

The worst thing! There was a little aquarium
near his headquarters, and he found that the
careless man in charge of it had not barred the
door. Goodness knows how many rare fish
might have been swept away in the rain!

Jimmy McGee bolted the door tightly and
then zoomie-zoomied home. Never before had
he traveled as fast as he did now.

Was Little Lydia all right? She must be all
right. By now she must be the real, right do-
nothing Little Lydia again, as she had been when
he rescued her from Monstrous, before he had
turned her into an electrified bebopping doll.

Yet what about that stare in her eyes as
though she were mesmerized by something? It
seemed as though those electric blue eyes of
hers *could,* the way a real person could, see

something. The thought had been in the back of his mind all afternoon. So now, behold Jimmy McGee, rounds finished, returning to his headquarters in six-sixty time.

The high winds were whipping the waterfall away sideways from his entranceway, pitching the water somewhere else. A little water was spraying into his home, but not much...just enough to create a nice little shallow pool. Maybe when the storm was over, it would remain there. In it he could clean his tools and nuts and bolts...also his stovepipe hat!

He zoomie-zoomied in and went right up to the boulder where he had laid Little Lydia on its pale mossy pelt. But there was no sign of Little Lydia.

Little Lydia was gone!

10

Refugees!

Where was Little Lydia? Frantically Jimmy McGee checked from top to bottom and side to side and under the roots of trees, in every nook and cranny. No sign. He even looked where he kept his pipes filled with scrolls and writings, his "library." She might have somehow gotten into a pipe and pretended she was a scroll, not a doll! She was that smart.

But no. He returned over and over to the place on the flat rock where he had laid her and where, looking at her eyes, he was struck by what an electric blue they were. Still he found no sign of Lydia, the do-nothing doll.

But there were others here in his headquarters! One by one they had been coming from this cranny or that, land animals and birds, all refugees from the storm.

At first, all of them eyed Jimmy McGee with caution, even fear. But soon, realizing they had nothing to be afraid of, they began, one by one, to follow him around. He was like a pied piper now, with one of his little probing pipes in hand.

He called out, "Little Lydia, come out! Bebop! Say something! If you can bebop again, please say something. My headquarters are a camp now. Lots of refugees from Lobelia. We will all have *fun, funny fun!*"

There was no answer. She really might have had a relapse or even escaped out into the storm or goodness knows what.

"Amy's home now. Come back!" he implored. "She misses you."

No reply. He didn't see how she could have been stricken with the zoomie-zoomies again because his thunder and lightning bolt box was in his stovepipe hat.

"Ah-h," he thought. "One of these refugees must know something about where she is, even—dreadful thought—may have swallowed her whole! So now to examine carefully each one here, question each politely, for all *are* my guests and outside the weather is horrid."

Followed by his little refugees, and with the birds hovering above, he made his way back to the hollowed-out rock, which was his favorite seat. The rock wall of the cave made a perfect backrest. This was the solid rock chair that was like the throne of an ancient king.

Well, hello! It was occupied. A little snake was coiled up tightly in the hollowed-down seat part. You could not see her head. It was cozily tucked inside her coil. She lay in the middle of his throne like a coil of a child's bright-colored jump-rope.

"Move out of that seat, Snakey," said Jimmy McGee. "It happens to be *my* seat, where I do my scroll work and my polishing. Uncoil yourself and make yourself comfortable on the next rock. Now, just slither along to over there." He poked her gently with his banging pipe. Even then she did not stir.

So Jimmy McGee moved to his second-best seat, right next to Snakey, where he could keep an eye on her. Then he got a piece of paper from his bombazine bag and prepared to make a scroll. The name of this was to be "Refugees from Hurricane Lobelia in My Winter Headquarters: A List." He planned to have each refugee step forward and be listed. He would look each one over carefully, study from its shape whether he or she might have swallowed Little Lydia, or at least give him a clue as to her whereabouts.

Jimmy McGee knew how a speech should be made. He had banged the pipes of many senators who sometimes went down to their cellars to practice their important speeches and did not wish to be overheard by some newspaperman hoping for a scoop for that night's paper. Though all the birds and animals spoke in the language of their own species, still they got the gist of everything that was said from being in a cave with Jimmy McGee. Because he was magic, they all got a touch of magic. All understood one another. They understood also the bebop language that Jimmy McGee had made up and in which he wrote his records for his scripts and scrolls.

So Jimmy McGee began: "Refugees! Guests! I am Jimmy McGee, a plumber. Welcome to my winter headquarters, where you are safe from

the storm! Will each one of you step forward—
no shoving—or fly down and say who you are. I
want to make a list of you all. Then, when the
storm is over and you want to go home, I will
check you off the list and we will know that
nothing has happened to you while you are
guests here. Now, the listing. Snakey, of course,
heads the list." Snakey gave no sign of having
heard any of this speech. But Jimmy McGee
continued anyway.

SNAKEY: A pretty little snake. Will not uncoil. Suspicious character.

BEAVER: Building a dam at the entranceway. Not a suspicious character.

BADGER: Jealous of Beaver. Make him door-
man. Not a suspicious character, but might
know if Little Lydia had zoomie-zoomied out.

RACCOON: Beautiful tail. Fine for dusting.
Keep him busy.

SQUIRREL: Has no tail. Is ashamed.

Just then, interrupting the proceedings,
Beaver swept something into the entranceway
with his own flat tail!

"My tail!" said Squirrel. He clutched it in his two paws.

"I'll fix it for you later on," Jimmy McGee promised. "Now to continue.

"Birds," Jimmy McGee said, "fly or step forward, say who you are. This may be a long-lasting storm. We want to have fun while it is going on."

There was a hoot from some upper ledge. A small gray owl, about the color of the rock, flew off his ledge. But he would not come down. He said, "I am Owl. I don't like snakes big or little. I don't trust them, and they don't trust me. Tell that fellow beside you to unwind himself. I don't like it. Everybody else is doing what you are asking."

He was right. Jimmy made a note of this.

OWL: A wise bird. May know something. Question him further.

CARDINAL BIRD: Always singing his special song, "Tweet tweet-tweet." Won't come down either. Birds don't seem to like Snakey.

"Any more birds?" asked Jimmy McGee, for he had heard a fluttering up high on a ledge.

"What about that flurry up in the large bolt bin?"

A parrot, very beautiful, appeared. "Filibuster is my name," he said in a rasping voice. He stood up on the bin, cocked his head, and looked down on the others. He seemed to be laughing at some joke known only to himself. Then he said, *"Voilà!"* Obviously he spoke both English and French, perhaps other languages as well, the bebop code included.

Filibuster's shrill "Voilà!" echoed over and over throughout headquarters. Many besides Jimmy McGee wished he would keep still. But Jimmy did note that Filibuster eyed Snakey with extreme concentration. He decided to label him a suspicious character, which really meant, in this case, question Filibuster later at great length. So he wrote:

FILIBUSTER: A beautiful parrot. Speaks many languages. Suspicious character.

Suddenly a sopping wet red hen, terrified, came through the entranceway with such speed that you'd have thought she had had an electric shock! She knocked over the dam Beaver was trying to make out of pipes and nuts and bolts.

Beaver didn't care and began again. It was his habit.

"Beaver!" Jimmy McGee said firmly. "Don't let your dam keep people out. Watch out for refugees. Be polite. Let everybody in. I'll give you a copy of my guest list. Look at this poor red hen. She almost didn't get in! When the storm is over, you can check people off the list as they leave. But no one may leave until I say O.K. We are missing a very important treasure. Someone here may have it. I have to pass the word to you, say, 'O.K., he or she may go!' That will be when the fury of the storm, Lobelia, has subsided and has blown out to sea."

"Filibuster!" screamed the parrot who seemed to love the sound of his own voice, especially his name.

Well, Jimmy McGee's speech *had* been a long one. True. But they all had heard it, and they all eyed one another and wondered whether or not he or she was looking a thief in the eye, or vice versa. Also, they wondered, what is this great treasure that is missing?

The poor red hen! Jimmy McGee now turned his attention to her. Her eyes were half closed, the lids a grave white and looking like fake ones used by a circus performer. "She might have the pip," conjectured Jimmy McGee. He wrapped her in a piece of old black bombazine. With her eyelids half down, she was quite a mournful sight in that black cloak.

"A clown hen!" hooted Owl.

This ridicule roused Red Hen. She shook off the black shawl and was her own wet self again. She appeared to be recovering and scratched her ear while standing on one foot. This brought about a burst of applause!

Owl said, "I know she would like to be called 'Ms. Red Hen!' It has distinction."

"Welcome, Ms. Red Hen!" said Jimmy McGee. He would have tipped his stovepipe hat were it not that the box with the bolts of thunder and lightning in it might have a dazzling and perhaps not too welcome effect.

Since Ms. Red Hen had only just arrived, *she* certainly had not eaten Little Lydia or made away with her. On his list, he wrote:

MS. RED HEN: Very wet and flustery. In a bad mood...or anxious?

Jimmy regarded Ms. Red Hen curiously. Maybe she would lay an egg here soon now, maybe inside the coil of Snakey, usurping the ancient throne? That should interest Snakey and make her unwind and join in.

Ms. Red Hen gradually subsided, though she did maintain a quiet sort of cluck-clucking constantly. Her cluck-clucks and Filibuster's constant "Voilà"s were quite annoying to some. Nerves were getting edgy.

"Nothing is madder than a wet red hen," said Owl sagely. He flew down to the ledge above Jimmy McGee's temporary seat. Here he could keep an eye on Jimmy McGee's listings and suggest corrections. His reputation as being a wise old owl gave him this privilege, he thought. And Jimmy McGee did not take offense.

"Cluck, cluck-cluck, catawcut!" Ms. Red Hen said over and over.

"She means 'Pawtucket,' not catawcut," Owl explained to Jimmy McGee, "because she is a Rhode Island red."

But Jimmy did not change his entry and got aid from Filibuster, who screamed, "Voilà!" He was the one who liked to be the noisemaker, not a wet red hen or an owl!

The squabbling brought an unlisted member of the group out of hiding. This was Rabbit.

"Where were you when the listing of the animals was going on?" asked Jimmy McGee curiously. He didn't understand why he hadn't seen Rabbit. Perhaps suddenly, like a bolt out of the blue, as if from nowhere, Little Lydia would come out of hiding as Rabbit had!

"Hiding. Just hiding," said Rabbit shyly.

Rabbit had come from high up in his headquarters, near where Little Lydia had last been seen. So Jimmy McGee wrote:

RABBIT: Shy, very nice...still...quite plump. Suspicious character.

Where could she have been hiding? He'd scanned every possible nook and cranny. He liked Rabbit. Maybe she knew something, though? He couldn't see why she would swallow Little Lydia, hair and all, for Little Lydia looked like neither a carrot nor a piece of lettuce.

Whoever was guilty would come to his mind in a real, regular striking and electrifying way. And he might rescue Little Lydia from inside one of the refugees with some help, perhaps, from his thunder and lightning bolt box.

From somewhere a cricket chirped. His winter headquarters were full of surprises. Cricket had the sense not to come out with all these many potential cricket-eaters around. People's stomachs were rumbling. He stayed where he was, but he wanted to be on the list.

Jimmy McGee felt that not only Cricket but also some of the other little ones needed special protection. He said to Badger, "Badger, you be the policeman. Bop somebody, but not hard, if he or she gets the idea a cricket or anybody else would be a tasty treat!"

Badger was happy to have a job. Beaver was doing all the work, and he was jealous. He thumped his two little front paws three times on a rock to show what would happen to the bigger animals if they should hurt any of the smaller guests.

Jimmy McGee made another entry in his list.

CRICKET: Cheerful. Harmless.

Now to finish up the list. "You, over there in the pool," he said. He was speaking to a large bullfrog.

"Bar-room!" said Frog.

This startled everybody. Frog had a booming bass voice, and its echo resounded up and down and roundabout headquarters.

Rabbit covered her ears and hid in her niche.

Filibuster screamed, "Voilà!"

Ms. Red Hen liked the sound. "Cluck-cluck catawcut!" she squawked.

Everybody made some noise or other, including Cardinal Bird, who, to show his appreciation of something novel, loudly sang "Tweet tweet-tweet."

If Jimmy McGee had been a composer of symphonies instead of a plumber, what a great "Works in G Major" this would be!

"Bar-room!" Frog boomed again, as though in agreement.

Jimmy McGee put him on the list.

BULLFROG: Frog for short. Quite stout. Suspicious character with that huge mouth of his!

Now that seemed to be all. But just then in came something with such strength that it knocked Beaver's dam down again, and Badger tried to thump it with his little paws, which did no good. It landed with a tremendous splash in the shallow pool at the entranceway, which, until now, Frog had considered his territory. Frog got out in great haste, sat on a rock, and gave a terrific "Bar-room!" instead.

Whatever had shot in lay exhausted in the pool, occupying practically all of it. Many gathered around cautiously, for all were curious.

Jimmy McGee stood up. "Who are you?" he asked. "Welcome!"

The dark, shiny creature flashed some words on his sleek, slippery back: ELECTRIC EEL FROM THE WATERS OF URUGUAY, SPECIMEN 916 IN THE AQUARIUM. I WANT TO GO BACK THERE.

All these words he flashed in electric fashion on his shiny skin, for he did not talk; he wrote his sayings in electricity on his skin.

"Well!" said Jimmy McGee. He was somewhat astonished that an electric eel would arrive in the midst of a possible epidemic of electric bebops in his headquarters. "You'll fit in very nicely here. Brighten things up a bit!"

"Wouldn't Little Lydia love this! Right up her alley," he thought. He realized that with the coming of the electric eel, strange events were bound to take place in headquarters, but what he did not yet know. He put Eely on the list.

EEL: Eely, an electric eel from the aquarium. A puzzle.

Jimmy McGee had seen that door ajar at the aquarium and had banged it shut when he had zoomed home from 3017 Garden Lane. Eely must have already gotten out and probably had been, through all this wild storm, tossed hither and yon in the brook or some nearby pool. What else might have escaped? Ts! Ts! That careless caretaker of such an important landmark as the aquarium!

Silence had fallen over all the refugees with the advent of the electric eel, and they all awaited another communication writ in lovely letters on this strange creature's back. But Jimmy McGee was used to such phenomena, he himself and then Little Lydia being expert practitioners of this art.

Right away—no time to be lost—he had to solve the mystery of the disappearance of Little Lydia, find her, get her back to Amy. He was certain that someone here had the answer, but who? He had his suspicions.

The only refugee who had not stepped forward to be counted, listed, and inspected by him was Snakey. She was still coiled up tightly in the middle of Jimmy McGee's real and rightful seat. When he became a little tired, he would curl up in it and have a one-two secs' rest!

He gave Snakey a strong poke with his scroll pipe, but there she lay. She would not stir.

"Snakey!" said Jimmy McGee. "Unwind! Say who you are, as the others have. Enter in! Do a snake dance! We are going to have a party soon—when we have something to celebrate—and I hope that will come about very, very soon!"

No movement on Snakey's part.

Owl said in awe, "She is in a trance."

Everyone gathered around to see a snake in a trance. They had supposed she was a cushion in this fine, generous gentleman's headquarters. Now all eyed Snakey with their bright, beady eyes.

"What a poor sport she is!" said Badger. Others nodded in agreement.

No one knew why Jimmy McGee wanted Snakey to unwind, but they were on his side. They were all guests in his headquarters!

Filibuster said in disgust, "Voilà!"

Snakey didn't care even if she heard. She had her head tucked so deeply inside her pretty coil that it was nowhere to be seen. Jimmy McGee thought that maybe Little Lydia was deep inside Snakey's coil and not inside Snakey, so he went to the top of his throne and peered as far into the coil as he could.

"Bebop, Little Lydia!" said Jimmy McGee.

There was no bebop reply. But suddenly, as though a needle had been stuck in her, Snakey did rouse herself. She unwound just an inch or so, even raised her head, which she swayed round and round while flicking her tongue in and out. She grinned a wide grin.

She was a friendly little snake and a very young one. Though silent, she appeared to be laughing. Everyone there knew that the way most snakes hear was with their tongues, for they have no ears. Jimmy McGee thought she might never have heard him urge her to unwind, this being the first time she had even raised her head. She must have gotten the message from some other source!

Little Lydia! Jimmy McGee was certain now that she must be inside Snakey.

Snakey observed everybody curiously with her beady eyes and then pulled her head back down inside her coil. So that was the end of what anyone could see of Snakey right now.

It seemed cozy and peaceful inside headquarters. Now and then Eely made things brighter by flashing a word on his shining back in a strange and foreign language. Maybe he was giving the news or telling about life in the aquarium? The refugees, scattered here and there, found the lights pretty anyway.

Outside, the storm was beginning to abate somewhat. Soon it might end and the guests depart. Jimmy McGee just had to find Little Lydia before the refugees went away.

He said, "Now we know who everybody is. Now the fun part of the party will begin. Make music, all of you. Let's have dancing and songs, charades...whatever." *Fun* was Little Lydia's favorite word. He thought it might bring a response.

"Fun!" Jimmy bebopped.

There was again a stir from somewhere inside Snakey.

"Let the party begin! Let the one who first took refuge here lead off. Who *was* the first? Eh?"

"Who-oo-oo was the first?" echoed Owl.

Filibuster said, "Voilà!"

11

The Party

Who *had* been the first refugee here?

The refugees eyed one another. Some wanted to have been the first and so would lead the dance. Others, the shy ones, like Rabbit, were glad not to have to lead off, not knowing the steps, though they would try to follow suit. Ms. Red Hen would have loved to lead off, but she could not even pretend to have been the first one in. Everyone knew that wet and flustery, and possibly with the pip, she had blown in later.

Then spoke Owl. All listened carefully, put a paw or a claw behind their ears, not to miss one single wise word.

Said Owl, "I thought that I was the first one here because when I blew in, I did not see one single soul. I flew to this ledge, and I fluffed up my wet feathers." He gave an example of how he had done this. "*Then*, suddenly from way up there, from deep inside that flat ledge and close to the wall, I suppose, there slithered out"— here he gave a dramatic pause, and everyone held his breath—"Snakey! And there she is!" He pointed at her, but she paid no attention, her hearing apparatus tucked down inside her coil.

Owl went on to say more to the breathless assemblage. "She slithered over to that choice rock, where she then coiled herself, looking like a pinwheel on the Fourth of July about to be lighted and go phizzing round and round. That, of course, as you see, did not happen, for there on that choice rock she still is! Therefore, Snakey was first, I second. I am sorry not to have had the honor to give a grand 'Hoo-oot!' when Mr. McGee might clap his hands and say, 'Let the Grand March commence!'" Then this learned Owl added, "By the way, she is a hoop snake. That's why she doesn't have better manners!"

Before Jimmy McGee ever zoomied off to Amy's house, he certainly had noted that Little Lydia was staring at something on the nearby rock with those electric blue eyes of hers. But there was nothing unusual about that. She was always just staring, and it depended on how she was lying. Sometimes one might think she was staring at something special. Maybe she *had* noticed Snakey. Or perhaps Snakey had come in right after he had left and before the rains came and found herself that nice high ledge to rest on, safe from rain and wind.

That was it! She had not been up on that ledge when Jimmy McGee left. He was impressed with Owl's accurate account of Snakey and of her slithering down to his throne. He just must see the whole of Snakey! She must know something very important about the whereabouts of lost Little Lydia! He had a strong suspicion about those whereabouts now.

"Snakey!" coaxed Jimmy McGee. "Please uncoil yourself. Stand up! Owl says you were the first one here. You have the honor to be the leader of the Grand March!"

Jimmy McGee saw that he might as well be talking to a wall. He had to persuade Snakey to raise her head and stick out her little tongue in order to hear him. Maybe help would come as before. He bopped Snakey gently with his small but most powerful bopping pipe and thought he heard a faint *"Fun! Funny fun!"*

That proved it. "Little Lydia is inside of Snakey! I must get her out!" he said to himself.

Again help came from within, for the coil gave a slithery wriggle. Snakey raised her head! "O-o-h, that's fine!" encouraged Jimmy McGee. Then before Snakey's head and her hearing apparatus could tuck itself back in the coil, Jimmy McGee said, "An honor is being bestowed upon you! Unwind completely! You are to be the leader of the Grand March of the Refugees!

"Do your pretty snake dance! Owl says you are a hoop snake! What a distinction! You probably have many talents. But all the refugees are watching you...their leader! Everyone will do some special thing, but I imagine you will outshine them all!"

All the refugees gathered around and fastened their eyes on Snakey. Would she unwind? If she did, they could see how long she was. If she were very long, they would make haste back to their own ledge and watch, not dance.

Snakey did not unwind, but she did raise her head a little higher.

"Ah!" said Jimmy McGee. "That's great." He gave his own head a shake to make sure his famous thunder and lightning bolt box was safe and sound up there in his stovepipe hat...to be used only in an emergency.

Snakey unwound a little more. She raised her head still higher. All could see it very well. It was pretty. She did a graceful dance movement with just her head, turning it almost all the way around and pleasing everybody with her wide grin. She was a friendly little snake. She looked to be laughing, as though she were having fun.

She flicked her little tongue out so that now she could hear and appreciate the applause. She was a very little hoop snake, perhaps only a few months old, and blown away from her family! Or from the zoo.

"My!" said Jimmy McGee. "If dancing with only your head is this pretty, how pretty the whole of you must look in a full-length dance! On the tip of your tail, for instance! Wouldn't we all like to see that! Wouldn't we, people?" He appealed to his guests. "Clap! Clap! Everybody clap!" implored Jimmy McGee.

Filibuster said shrilly, "Voilà!" Everyone clapped in his or her own way. "Tweet tweet-tweet," sang Cardinal Bird. Beaver slapped his flat tail on the entrance rock. So did Badger with his not-flat tail. Squirrel threw nuts and bolts around like acorns. They didn't hit anyone—he was careful of that. Raccoon and Squirrel waved their tails.

Too bad that one of Squirrel's nuts had not hit Snakey...not hard, but just hard enough to keep her awake and be part of Jimmy McGee's "stand-up-straight" plan. But Snakey, still grinning amiably, just tucked her head inside her colorful coil and seemed about to go to sleep again.

Jimmy McGee was exasperated. When would he ever be able to see whether or not she had a bulge inside of her? The Little Lydia bulge and where in Snakey it was? It seemed to him that he heard a murmur inside Snakey like the rumbling of a person's stomach who has indigestion, or...but, it couldn't be...a faraway faint rumbling of thunder. He checked his hat. Bolt box still up there safe and sound.

Jimmy McGee decided the party must go on, whether or not they had a spoilsport in their midst. The first refugee, Snakey, who was supposed to lead the Grand March, was tucking her head away again. "Owl," said Jimmy McGee. "You were the second one here. Please be the substitute Grand March leader, the stand-in."

But now Owl did not want the honor. Said he would rather be the Commentator.

In the end it was Badger. He was already a sort of policeman. Jimmy McGee gave him a banging pipe, which he was to bang three times if anyone went on too long with their solo or recitation. So now he was like an orchestra leader, and everybody made music.

Badger was a marvelous march leader. Jimmy McGee felt things would go on splendidly while he put into effect a very great idea he had had. It involved a way to get Snakey to stand up straight and be inspected.

Everyone was busy and had joined in except Snakey, and of course Eely, who couldn't; he *had* to stay in the water. However, he contributed to the festivities in a beautiful fashion. He flashed his electric lights on and off, making the cave very pretty; a musical behind a little waterfall in Mount Rose Park!

"Just like the lights on old Broadway," observed Raccoon, who had spent some time in a park in the area.

"Right," said Owl.

Then everybody wanted to talk or sing or do a dance all at once. But suddenly Ms. Red Hen, as though to cap the climax, gave a loud "cluck-cluck catawcut," stood up, walked around—though no one had said "Encore" to her long speech about the ancestry of Rhode Island reds—hopped up on a ledge across the dance floor from Snakey, and laid an egg! A hurricane egg! Cheers went up from all over headquarters, both for Ms. Red Hen and for Eggy.

All this hullabaloo and shouts of "Hurrah!" aroused even Snakey from her torpor. She eyed Ms. Red Hen's ledge with great interest; and she grinned her wide, wide grin and flicked her tongue to right and to left. Ms. Red Hen covered her hurricane egg completely with her wings and spread herself over it so widely that she was as big as two hens. No one was going to get even a peek at Eggy...certainly not beady-eyed Snakey!

"Well, now is the time," Jimmy McGee reluctantly decided, "to make use of my thunder and lightning bolt box!" He was not going to open it. It was still in his stovepipe hat and was going to stay there. He was just going to see if, by being very close to it, it would have an electrifying effect on Snakey.

Jimmy McGee placed his stovepipe hat with his treasured bolt box in it on the seat close to Snakey. He said, "Snakey! Now that you have had such a deep slumber midst all the partying, how would you like to do a little hoop-snake dance around and around my elegant stovepipe hat? No one else come close, please," he implored his guests. "She may be shy!"

Snakey flicked her tongue against the stovepipe hat with its precious thunder and lightning bolts inside. The effect on her was terrific! With her "hearing aid" tongue, Snakey heard a strange sound, which was electrifying to her!

She rose up and balanced herself on the stovepipe hat by just the slender tip end of her tail! She swayed and swayed and did the noted snake dance, such as few have ever seen, and all the while she was grinning and flicking her tongue to right and to left.

"Listening to the music," explained Owl. "And," said the wise owl, "she is a hoop snake. Remember that, and do not be surprised at what she may do next!"

The refugees were stunned at the sight of this

remarkable performance. They drew back a little, not knowing much about hoop snakes, even such a tiny one as this, and in spite of what Owl said, knew they would be surprised at what Snakey might do next.

Jimmy McGee saw, and so did all the refugees, that halfway down in the beady-eyed, swaying snake, there was a bulge, not big, but still a bulge!

"Where there is one bulge, there could easily be two," the littlest ones thought. They hid in nearby bins.

Ms. Red Hen smiled appreciatively at Snakey's dance. She did suggest that, besides Eggy, there might be another addition to the refugee camp... a little Snakey?

She was just as happy as everybody else, however, to hear Beaver say he would check the guest list carefully to make sure the bulge inside Snakey was not one of the refugee regulars.

"Here! All here!" reported Beaver.

"Here, all here, of course," thought Jimmy McGee, who was positive he knew what the bulge in Snakey was...Little Lydia! But now, how to get her out of Snakey?

Then a gasp went up from the entire population, for in bright electric letters a sign appeared

on Snakey as she swayed this way and that on the rock throne of Jimmy McGee.

The sign said: JIMMY MCGEE . . . HERO . . . BEBOP TO ME!

"A miracle!" said Owl. But he drew back to join the rest of the guests huddling in the rear and wondering, "What next?"

The sign came on, and the sign went off . . . the same sign: JIMMY MCGEE . . . HERO . . . BEBOP TO ME!

Snakey swayed and swayed and, on her tippy-tail, danced her snake dance. She made some people dizzy.

"Voilà!" said Filibuster nervously.

To Jimmy McGee, one thing was certain. The bulge in the beady-eyed, electrified Snakey was Little Lydia, the little lost do-nothing doll. Now how to get her out? How?

He addressed the refugees. "There is a prisoner inside our guest, Snakey. She must be rescued. But how?"

"How? How?" echoed voices through the winter headquarters.

A very faint sound, like a bebop word, echoed also from inside Snakey. *"How?"*

12

The Bulge in the
Beady-eyed Snake

Jimmy McGee had to act right now! Little Lydia was sending him a bebop message! So while Snakey was balancing herself on her tippy tail on top of Jimmy McGee's stovepipe hat with his rare little thunder and lightning bolts inside it, Jimmy McGee thought up his plan. He said in bebop code:

*Little Lydia, if you are the bulge in the
 snake I see,*
Bebop, bebop a message to me.

Right away came the bebop answer:

I'm in the Snake;
I think I'll bake!

The refugees heard the bebops but did not completely comprehend the code. They knew it had something to do with the bulge in the beady-eyed snake. But what? Squirrel nervously dropped a nut from Bin No. 9. It struck Jimmy McGee's stovepipe hat, became all charged with electricity, and bounded right back up to him.

"Strange goings-on here," said Squirrel, and cuddled up to Raccoon.

Grinning widely, Snakey continued her tip-of-the-tail dance.

"Get me out, Jimmy McGee!" came the bebops. *"Get me out!"*

Everyone saw that with these words the bulge had begun to move.

"Digesting what she ate," said Owl sagely. Then he added, "Well, will you look at that, will you?"

Along with her bebop words, Little Lydia had an old-time attack of the zoomie-zoomies inside of Snakey. This made Snakey wriggle this way and that and then suddenly rise up into the air, off of the stovepipe hat completely, and shoot straight up to the topmost reaches of headquarters!

For a while she seemed to be suspended up there and to be dancing on zigzag stilts like pale streaks of lightning. She was doing what Little Lydia used to do back in summer headquarters!

This was a pretty sight but unsettling to some of the refugees, especially to Cardinal Bird, who had considered himself safe from all these shenanigans high up on his ledge. He did not sing his song right now. But Ms. Red Hen, her beak hanging open as she strained to keep track of Snakey and at the same time guard Eggy, suggested that Eely, from the aquarium, had passed on his electricity to poor little Snakey, a very young little hoop snake at that.

Others thought this might be Eely himself. But no. That fellow was too big. And anyway, there he was lying in his pool, much too shallow for him, but at least it was water. Also, he was flashing his own neon lights on and off, giving over and over his name and birth and source of origin—exactly what it said about him on the description over his pool in the aquarium.

Fortunately, he was very young, or he would not have fit in here at all.

"A competition!" exclaimed Ms. Red Hen and cackled with delight. "Electric eel in pool. Electrified snake doing high jinks in the loft! Cluck!"

"There's magic going on here," said Owl

sagely. "Our host is a magician. See what else is inside that hat? A rabbit next, perhaps?"

"I'm already out, never was in," said Rabbit. She was so nervous that she hid behind a rock; but soon, unwilling to miss some other curious display, she came out.

Then down spun Snakey, who began to wind herself into a tight little coil again, this time on top of the hat, not as comfortable, but she didn't seem to care, for she didn't know what was inside that hat nor would it have mattered. Something was bothering her stomach.

Jimmy McGee said coaxingly, "Stand up straight just once more, please, Snakey. Then you can coil and uncoil as much as you want."

Snakey seemed to get a nudge from inside, for she looked herself over.

"Now!" said Jimmy McGee. "Coil yourself slowly...slowly, oh, so slowly...but tightly around and around my handsome stovepipe hat, which I now lend to you to add wonderment to this party. Begin with the tippy-tip end of you. There is a bulge in you. All the refugees can bear witness to this. You have swallowed something that is not in your line at all. If you do as I say, winding, oh, so tightly around my rare, hand-hewn stovepipe hat, you may force the little thing—whatever it is—up! And then, it will pop right out of your mouth!"

Swaying prettily on her tippy tail, Snakey eyed Jimmy McGee, and she grinned, for she could hear what he said.

But the bulge seemed to have gone in deeper! Dismayed, Jimmy McGee said, "Ts! Ts!"

Suddenly Bullfrog boomed out, "Snakey! Have you had something to eat that no one else here had even a bite of? If so, what? You have had refreshments. We'd like some, too!"

"In a refugee camp, you are supposed to share the provisions," Owl added firmly.

"What's that bulge in you anyway?" asked Badger bluntly. "Come clear, now!" He brandished his banging pipe.

Jimmy McGee said, "Don't bother Snakey! She's having enough trouble as it is getting what she has eaten down or up. Look at the way she's behaving! Would any of the rest of you like to have to behave that way? Swallow something that bebops and shoots you like a skyrocket to the top of my headquarters?"

No one did like that idea, and the grumbling ceased.

"Indigestion," suggested Ms. Red Hen. "The pip!"

Jimmy McGee tapped his stovepipe hat with one of his small banging pipes. "Come on now, Snakey!" he said. "You swallowed something that was not good for you. Do what I said, and out it will pop!"

Snakey paused, swaying prettily...

"Wind!" urged Jimmy McGee.

From inside Snakey there came a bebop echo. *"Wind!"*

And Snakey obliged. Beginning at the tip end of her tail, she began slowly, very slowly but surely, to wind herself tightly around Jimmy McGee's stovepipe hat. The narrow brim made a fine balance for this venturesome exhibition. She looked like a colorful jump rope beginning to be wound round and round a belaying pin on the deck of some strange boat.

Everyone watched tensely. They crowded closely in front of Snakey not to miss one single thing. A cheer went up as Snakey made the first go-round!

"Voilà!" screamed Filibuster.

Pausing for a moment to look at them all, and with the rest of her lithe body swaying gracefully, little Snakey flicked her tongue in and out and grinned as though she appreciated the applause. Then she started her next go-round. Now, here she was, coming round the bend again!

Rabbit, who was used to races, became an umpire. "Now," she said, her nose all a-quiver, "she's coming round the bend again!"

"Two coils of Snakey round the stovepipe hat now!" shouted Badger. Snakey's coils were as neat and tight as those on a spool of fine thread!

"Bravo! Bravo!" Headquarters echoed the bravos all up and down and around.

"Tweet tweet-tweet!" sang Cardinal Bird.

Snakey started round again. With each go-round, when she came in sight, she stretched the whole rest of herself out toward her cheering audience, as though to say, "How'm I doing?" Then she flicked her tongue out of her wide, happy mouth before commencing the next go-round.

"Doesn't want to get dizzy," said Ms. Red Hen. "That's why she stops and stares after each go-round."

"Maybe she is measuring herself to see if all of her will fit," suggested the practical Badger.

Beaver nodded. "I think she'll fit, she's so small," he said. He was a builder and should know.

But with the next go-round, everyone could

see that Snakey had reached the odd bulge in her middle. This was a problem! Now, she would have to wind herself even more tightly. Otherwise there was going to be a lumpy look to the coil, which until now had been so perfect! This tightness might, just might, *force* the bulge, whatever *it* was, *"Out!"*

That *out* had come from the thing inside!

Suddenly, whatever it was that Snakey had swallowed lighted up. It shone brightly through Snakey's skin! Of course Jimmy McGee knew that this was because the bulge had now reached the thunder and lightning bolt box inside his hat!

Even Jimmy McGee was excited at the amazing effect that this go-round had produced. Tiny zigzag streaks of lightning shone through Snakey's skin. If this kept up, Jimmy McGee's elegant hat would be transformed into some strange hat, perhaps a shako? Or a fez? Very loud bebops echoed through the cave. Faint rumblings of thunder also echoed through the cave. Snakey looked eerie, and what was in her sounded eerie, too.

Everyone drew back in awe!

"Let me out!" came the bebops, louder and louder.

"Whatever Snakey ate, she ate it alive!" observed Owl wisely. He had a scowl on his face. "And it's still alive!" he added. He truly must have great wisdom to understand this odd occurrence.

The curiosity of the refugees drew them like a magnet to the Snakey-trimmed hat of Jimmy McGee, who alone knew that the bulge must be Little Lydia!

Everyone had to see what was going to happen. Something was bound to, for with each go-round the bulge was slowly but surely being forced toward Snakey's mouth...still happily grinning.

"Snakey may have eaten a whole swarm of lightning bugs," suggested Ms. Red Hen.

"Lightning bugs are out of season," said Owl.

"And they don't bebop," chirped a little voice from up high. This was Cricket. It was his first comment and drew attention. Some of the refugees clapped.

"Snakey may be a new species of snake altogether," suggested Beaver, taking a minute off now and then from building another dam to get a glimpse of the goings-on around the hat...a new spectacle entirely from any in his experience.

"Voilà!" exclaimed Filibuster, who wished he had thought this up. But he was a good sport, and he agreed. "Yes," he said. "One not yet listed in books...electric bebopping hoop snake!"

Owl also, being the wise one, put in, "Electric eel, yes! We even have one of those among our guests. But I agree with Filibuster. Electric bebopping hoop snake...a freak. Still, in all fairness, we must agree we are not certain of the 'hoop' part yet. Only time will tell, and very soon. If so, in the books it may say, 'Only electric hoop snake known to mankind so far was first noted in the headquarters of a plumber by the name of Mr. John McGee in Washington, D.C.'"

Ms. Red Hen, tired of all this learned discussion, wanted to watch what was going on at the stovepipe hat and wished she could cluck "Filibuster!" and bring an end to his and Owl's learned discourses. She shoved her way closer to the center of attraction.

The twists Snakey was making around the hat were becoming slower and slower. Of course, Jimmy McGee knew that the bulge was Little Lydia. Being so close to his thunder and lightning bolt box, she had become recharged by its electricity.

"Quiet!" he commanded. "Everybody be quiet. The bulge speaketh now!"

"Get me out of here, you, Jimmy McGee! You!" And she added, *"Or I'll never speak to you ever again! So there!"*

"Soon!" promised Jimmy McGee in bebop code language. "You're nearing the finish now. Another go-round by Snakey and you will be at the exit. Then it will be zoomie-zoomie time again for you and for me!"

Ms. Red Hen said, "What'd I tell you? Or rather, Beaver tell you?" For she was honest and gave credit where credit was due. "A new species...an electric bebopping hoop snake! Cluck, cluck-cluck, catawcut!" But she went on, "That's her vocal box, that thing that Snakey's got in there. That's what it is. And it got out of place...belongs up there where it is now. Don't tongue and cheek go together? If she were the old-fashioned type of snake, she would hiss. That's what snakes do...hiss...not grin and get bulges. Cluck!" she said, disgusted, and clawed the hard rock with her foot to show her disgust.

"We may all be a new species before we get out of here," said Bullfrog grumpily. "Maybe I'm already a new species and don't know it. If I'm not a frog, what am I? A bull?"

This idea made Frog laugh...a huge, enormous laugh! His mouth was open very, very wide! He threw back his head and let out a deafening "Bar-room!" His throat puffed in, and it puffed out. His laughter was so catching that everybody had to join in. All kinds of laughter echoed through headquarters.

Frog could not stop laughing. "I'm a bully-frog!" he panted. He held onto his belly. Breathing in a tremendous amount of air, he threw back his head, opened wide his mouth, and let forth an extraordinary "Bar-room!"

Laughter of all sorts continued to echo in the cave!

Still the greatest attraction was Snakey, and attention was mainly upon her and her bulge.

Frog started another deep, rolling bar...that much came out...but, exactly at that moment, Snakey completed her last go-round on the stovepipe hat of Jimmy McGee! Whatever the bulge was, it sped out with such speed, like a bolt out of the blue, that it landed, as though aimed there, right in the wide open mouth of guffawing Frog!

"My! Oh, my!" exclaimed Jimmy McGee in dismay. "Out of the frying pan into the fire!"— for it *was* Little Lydia in her calico dress and with her frizzy hair who had been shot straight from Snakey's grinning mouth into Frog's wide open mouth!

"What now, what next?" pondered Jimmy McGee. "Harder to get Little Lydia out of a bullfrog than having Snakey do the snake dance round and round my stovepipe hat!"

But Jimmy McGee did not have to worry long, for everything that was happening went on at great speed! Frog, having already said the first half, the "bar" part of his gigantic "Barroom," finished the great roaring second half of his guffaw before Little Lydia could get stuck in his throat and be gulped down into his fat, quivering belly!

That sent Little Lydia zooming back out again! Sending off electric sparks right and left, she leaped from one refugee to another. Because of her light touch wherever she happened to land, each refugee caught a minor case of the thunder-and-lightning-bolt zigzags.

"Voilà!" exclaimed Filibuster and turned a somersault!

13

The Grand Jamboree

What confusion there was now in winter headquarters! A real epidemic of the zoomie-zoomies was rampant here in Jimmy McGee's domain.

"Fun! Fun! Funny fun!" bebopped Little Lydia as she sped up and down and here and there. No one could keep up with her, not even Filibuster, who hoped to add a new word to his vocabulary but was instead stricken with such a charge of electricity that all he could do was scream, "Voilà!" sixty-six times and turn somersaults.

Before Jimmy McGee's hat could bounce off his throne and roll away, take on a life of *its* own, Jimmy McGee grabbed it, made sure his thunder and lightning bolts were safely stored in it, and popped it firmly on his head. There his precious bolts were going to stay until he wanted to let them go, and that was not now!

When he caught Little Lydia, he would put her in his bombazine bag, so she would not be recharged in any way by the magic bolt box!

Naturally Snakey, having harbored Little Lydia inside of her for such a long time and also having been so close to the thunder and lightning bolt box in Jimmy McGee's hat while doing her rounds, had the most severe case of the zoomie-zoomies! Now she, too, could be free to enter in the fun!

All tried to control their magic powers for a moment to look at Snakey, who had already proven herself to be the most gifted performer here while she had the Little Lydia bulge inside of her! But now she surpassed herself! She grabbed the tip end of her tail in her grinning mouth, made herself into a hoop, and rolled round and round, a trick that run-of-the-mill ordinary hoop snakes do not often do!

As Snakey rolled past Badger, he gave her a gentle swipe with his banging pipe, and round and round she rolled. She bounced from ledge to ledge. At first just Badger gave the gentle little swat that kept Snakey rolling. But now, all the refugees took part in the game of "keep-our-hoopy-snake-a-rolling!" All gave her a gentle push as she passed and did keep her spinning round and round.

"A pinwheel fireworks," said Owl. His fluffy brown feathers had gone zigzag!

Cardinal Bird sang "Tweet tweet-tweet" as he flew through Snakey, creating a spectacle especially beautiful because he was such a brilliant red!

"Fun! Fun! Funny fun!" bebopped Little Lydia and hopped through Snakey over and over again.

Everyone crowded around trying to follow Snakey and to jump through her. Faster and faster she rolled, bouncing from ledge to ledge, so jumping through her was hard.

"Line up! Line up! Take turns!" shouted Badger, who thought he was still in charge.

Beaver was quivering with excitement, but he was too conscientious to leave his post, even though his fur had zigzags and sparkled from the zoomie-zoomies that were affecting everyone, some more, some less. Beaver hoped that, even though he was the doorkeeper, he would be able also to have his turn of jumping through Snakey!

First came Filibuster...impatient. It really wasn't fair because he had already been through once. But all was forgiven, for he was such a beautiful sight and able, even while jumping, to scream "Voilà! Voilà!"

Jimmy McGee scolded him, though. "Yield the floor to the next in line!" he said firmly.

This happened to be Ms. Red Hen.

Ms. Red Hen had been reluctant to leave her egg and join the happy hoop-snake game, but she couldn't resist. She asked Cardinal Bird to mind Eggy for a moment, and uttering a "cluck, cluck, catawcut," she fluttered through Snakey. This was not easy, for Snakey was rolling faster and ever faster! There should be a prize for the champion hoop-snake jumper who had gone through the most times!

"Fun! Fun! Funny fun!" bebopped Little Lydia. She zoomie-zoomied over to Eggy, where she alighted briefly, and then zoomied off somewhere else, zigzagging around and having a wonderful time.

Ms. Red Hen was filled with pride, having

hurled herself through Snakey while she was spinning as fast as a fireworks pinwheel! Ms. Red Hen's feathers crackled as loudly as she cackled while she fluttered back to Eggy!

But instead of Eggy, out stepped a chick, having pecked her shell wide open with the zoomie-zoomie speed she had caught from Little Lydia. After her first astonishment, Ms. Red Hen grabbed the shell, which was in fair condition, to take home with her, if she could manage. She would then lord it over the other stick-at-home hens, keep it as a souvenir, and recount the curious occurrence of the bursting forth of Hurricane Eggy.

"Marvels of science!" observed Owl.

Ms. Red Hen clucked with delight over her chicky, who was growing in zoomie-zoomie time and already had delicate zigzag feathers. Encouraged by Ms. Red Hen, who wanted to brag about her if they ever got home to the barnyard, Chickie followed her mother, who cluck-clucked constantly and egged her on to make the jump through Snakey. She did it! Everybody cheered!

Then Chickie and her mother zoomed up to some high ledge to watch what came next.

Squirrel was next. "Don't I get a turn?" he

said plaintively. He was still clinging to his Hurricane Lobelia tail. It wasn't on him, but he was clutching it tightly in his two little front paws as he leaped through Snakey. Alas! He dropped his tail. But a miracle happened! In falling, his tail had caught an electric charge from Little Lydia as she sped by, and it landed with such an impetus on Squirrel that it attached itself firmly exactly where it belonged. Once through Snakey, Squirrel turned around and saw what had happened. Astonished, he tried to give his tail a twitch. It twitched! It was on a little crooked,

but it was his real, right squirrel tail again, and even could make a pretty curve like a question mark!

"Hurricane Lobelia tail-survival incident," said Squirrel proudly.

"It looks distinguished, Mr. Squirrel," said Ms. Red Hen kindly. "You and I have lent great fame to this refugee camp! Me...Eggy! You... your tail restored!"

"Voilà!" exclaimed Filibuster.

Everybody clapped and said, "Hooray for hurricane squirrel tail!"

The other refugees now had a turn jumping through Snakey. Some, Filibuster for one, had more than one loop-the-loop through the pinwheel circle. Only Eely from Uruguay, who could not leave his little pool, and Beaver, brave builder of the dam, were not able to join in and had to just watch and applaud.

The electrical effect of the bolt charges was waning, though now and then some refugee had a recurrence of the strange affliction and tottered absurdly or crawled through Snakey for one final fling.

However, Snakey, having had the most severe case, was still rolling around like a hoop, the tip of her tail still in her mouth. The rest of the tired refugees sat back drowsily and contented themselves with simply watching her. They began to long for home.

Jimmy McGee saw that Little Lydia's attack was wearing off, too. Just in time she tottered to the rock near Jimmy McGee's throne before she collapsed. Perhaps Little Lydia was getting back to being her real, right self. Her eyes were fastened seemingly on nothing. She and no other guest were anywhere near the thunder and lightning bolt box, safe and tightly clamped inside the stovepipe hat of Jimmy McGee.

Little Lydia did try to say something. She bebopped the words *"Jimmy McGee, hero..."* Then she remembered and added, *"...a little fellow, a plumber, a banger on pipes..."* But these words grew fainter and fainter and more like a whisper, an echo in a cave.

Jimmy McGee picked her up gently. She was still dressed in the blue-flowered calico dress she had had on when he had rescued her from Monstrous, and her electric blue eyes were focused on nothing and seeing nothing. He put her in his bombazine bag, which he slung over his shoulder. Everything was safe and sound now. He had his thunder and lightning bolt box in his hat ready for what was coming next, and he had a plan about that!

In his headquarters, festivities, hullabaloos, dancing, speeches were nearly over...just a few of the sturdy ones still trying to do a magical stunt, but to no avail. All were wobbly.

But outside?

Well, outside Hurricane Lobelia was over. She hadn't stayed long. Here in Washington,

D.C., they had just gotten the edge of it. While Jimmy McGee had been having songs, parties, electrical walks, and Snakey high jinks, the wind and the rain had stopped. No longer was water splashing over Beaver's dam and keeping Eely good and wet! And nowhere else in headquarters had any water seeped in. Now the little waterfall was falling straight down, not being swept off to Dunbarton Oaks or somewhere!

"Be prepared for the exodus," said Jimmy McGee to Beaver, keeper of the dam.

"I am ready," said Beaver, quivering with his importance. He had the guest list in his hands to check people off as they left. "But," he said wistfully, "I never had a chance to jump through the hoop snake!"

"You still may," Jimmy McGee assured him. "Snakey still has the tip of her tail in her mouth. And she is still rolling around slowly . . . slowly. Check the guests off your list as they depart. Women and children first. So Ms. Red Hen and Chickie should be the first ones out. Though she grew fast because of the magic, Chickie is still a baby!"

Now Beaver was happy. He began to take down his dam of nuts and bolts. He could build himself a real, right beaver dam of twigs and roots and branches, an old shoe, anything that floated by down the brook a ways.

Jimmy McGee stood up on his own special rock chair, his throne. A plumber usually, not a speechmaker, Jimmy McGee was now about to make a speech.

"Attention! My friends...guests..." he said. "The party is over. Hurricane Lobelia has blown out to sea. Now the sky is a beautiful deep blue. You are freed from the terror of high winds and rain. You may go home now.

"Everybody queue up at the entranceway, everybody. No more bulges in Snakey. Beaver will check you off the list as you leave. Thank you for coming. You were wonderful guests! Each one of you was wonderful. Don't wait for the next hurricane to visit me. So now, my friends, line up!"

Although Jimmy McGee's farewell address was rather long, it did not seem so because he gave it in the bebop way. Each one said, "Thank you," in his or her own special zoomie bebop way, the magic of this rare condition lingering on.

Then they lined up for the exodus parade with Ms. Red Hen and little Chickie beside her in the lead. No one was jealous of her. She had been so spectacular, laying an egg just like that in the middle of a hurricane and in curious surroundings! Squirrel was the last in line. The zoomie-zoomies had really helped his tail, which he waved like a plume. It still had some soft golden zigzags in its fur, which might be there forever more.

Raccoon was not jealous. His bushy tail was spectacular enough already and did not need any improvement.

But now, suddenly Snakey, in a final burst of the magic still within her, rolled over to the entranceway just a second before the exodus began and suspended herself on a jagged root right behind the little waterfall. There she swung prettily in the breeze.

Everybody clapped, and as each guest left, he or she now had one last leap through Snakey, still with her tail in her mouth, still lighting up like pinwheel fireworks. The force of their leaps landed them on the other side of the waterfall. They zoomied through so fast that Beaver had trouble keeping track of them.

Even Eely made it through with a boost from Beaver. After all, he was little more than a baby electric eel, or he would not have been acquired by the keepers of the aquarium. Into the brook he made it, beyond the waterfall, but the water was not as warm as he would have liked. He was bound to reach warmer waters in the South, however, by means of his own brand of electricity unless, of course, the keepers of the aquarium were on the lookout for him and had perhaps even caught him before the exodus ended.

"Quién sabe?" said Filibuster, who had picked up that word, new to him, during the party from Eely himself. Eely had flashed it on his back, and Filibuster saw it and put it in his repertoire.

Jimmy McGee shouted a warning. "Everybody help everybody!"

He need not have said a word, for Ms. Red Hen, standing on a rock on the far side of the brook, with Chickie beside her, turned, looked through the sparkling waterfall at Jimmy McGee, and said, "Mr. McGee. We all thank you. We have formed a club. We...all of us, and all our descendents hereafter...hereby establish a society named Refugees from Hurricane Lobelia in the Headquarters of Mr. Jimmy McGee.

"Our headquarters are going to be in the gardener's tool shed in Dunbarton Oaks Park, right across the brook. Those who like the water may stay outside, in or out of the brook. Those who like trees can perch in them and sing 'Tweet tweet-tweet' early in the morning. And those who care for neither can come into the gardener's shed with Chickie and me.

"Owl already knows that shed. Filibuster does, too. Some senators practice speeches there; otherwise it is very quiet! Cluck-cluck, catawcut!" she exclaimed as her grand finale.

"Voilà!" screamed Filibuster. Nevertheless, he sped from tree to tree to Ms. Red Hen's distinguished headquarters. Knowing the shed, he wanted to take immediate possession of his favorite listening perch.

Now only Beaver and Snakey were left. Snakey was still swaying in the entranceway and enjoying a mist from the waterfall that cooled her off somewhat. Also she liked the reflection of herself in the sunlit waterfall, so she swang and swang. Now Beaver had his chance after all to jump through her! He handed Jimmy McGee his list of guests. He said, "All are accounted for except for myself and Snakey.

So, will you please check us off, Snakey and me, when we go?"

Then Beaver plunged through Snakey, not only the famous little hoop snake herself, but also her reflection in the waterfall. Right away he headed downstream, where he soon caught up with the others.

Now Snakey was the last to leave the camp of the refugees. "You were the best, Snakey," said Jimmy McGee. "You kept Little Lydia safe and sound for me all through Hurricane Lobelia at a time when she was most afflicted with magic. You kept the party moving...rolling, I should say. Everyone had a good time. Maybe I'll see you again some day, perhaps during the next hurricane to hit these parts, or just for a visit to your friends up yonder, the other side of the brook."

Snakey slowly let the tip of her tail slip out of her mouth. She grinned at Jimmy McGee. It was a sort of comradeship. She then slithered away and disappeared in the direction of the gardener's tool shed in Dunbarton Oaks Park.

There they were all having so much to do! All had to build new homes. How fast Beaver was piling things up! "Much more elegant than nuts and bolts," he muttered to Badger, who tried to help.

Too bad Jimmy McGee couldn't help! But he had a very important task to do...getting Little Lydia safely back home at last to Amy, the *Who's Who* writer, before anything else happened to her.

He was sure she was cured of that "Z" condition in Amy's book, cured completely. Safe she was still in his bombazine bag. The thunder and lightning bolt box was far, far away from her up in his stovepipe hat.

"Let's go!" he said. "Make ready for our last-time zoomie-zoomie ride!"

Little Lydia said nothing. Not even *"Fun!"*

A very little do-nothing doll again, at last. And himself, Jimmy McGee, a little fellow, a plumber, a banger on pipes...a hero? At last?

14

McGee, Jimmy: Hero!

Jimmy McGee stood for a moment on the other side of the waterfall. The whole world was washed clean and fresh after Lobelia. The sky was a deep, clear blue...not a cloud anywhere. The sun, about to set, was a lovely rose-red. There was a rainbow. He smiled. The refugees should try to jump through that!

But now did he ever have work to do! Even though the entire force of Hurricane Lobelia had not struck here, still there was much hard work ahead...wires down, trees blown over, and pipes out of order. But right now, the important, the most important, thing was to get Little Lydia back to Amy. Then he would be worthy of having the word *hero* tacked onto his name in the M's in Amy's *Who's Who Book.*

So with Little Lydia safe in the bombazine bag slung over his shoulder and with the thunder and lightning bolt box securely balanced in his stovepipe hat, he sped over to 3017 Garden Lane.

Down in the cellar, right under the narrow, dusty window that opened onto Garden Lane, he saw Amy's carton of toys and dolls and books. This carton had been the last one put in the old gray Dodge in Truro and the first to be hoisted out in front of 3017 Garden Lane and then dragged down into the cellar!

Here, on top of the box, just as it had been there in Truro, was Amy's little red-brown notebook, the *Who's Who Book,* which had Little Lydia's hand-crocheted blue shawl wrapped around it. Jimmy McGee started to open the book. But, as always, it opened itself to the page where he and Little Lydia were listed. "Lydia, Little: a teeny, tiny doll with bright blue eyes.... Can't walk, can't talk, can't say 'Mama.' Has bristly, curly, long golden hair.... Lost in the ocean. Captured by a Monstrous wave! But I hope she will be rescued by a Hero!"

A *hero*! The rescue part was right, but until Amy held this little doll in her hands, only that would make the hero part right. Well! That's what he hoped to do right now.

He took Little Lydia out of his bombazine bag and looked at her for one-two secs. "Well," he said. "Good-by, now. Don't get lost again. If you do, try to remember the bebops and the *fun* word. I'll hear you."

Then he placed her on the L and M page in Amy's *Who's Who Book.* When Amy came down to get her things and take them upstairs, Little Lydia would be the first thing she would see lying there on top of her book, with her little blue shawl beside her.

"Bye, then!" he said.

Little Lydia stared at the sooty ceiling. Cobwebs were in the corners, but she didn't see them or anything. So bright a blue her eyes were, though, that even in this dusky cellar they shone with their blueness. And her pretty flowered dress looked brighter than it had, perhaps because of all the curious adventures she had been through. But now she was truly a do-nothing doll again, no longer an electrified bebopping doll!

Jimmy McGee took one last look at her. Nuisance though she had been...think of all the things he had *not* done while he was busy trying to earn the name of being a hero...still he would miss Little Lydia more than a little...her and her bebops and her *"Get to work, lazy Jimmy McGee!"*

"Well, bye again," he said. And he sprang into action.

He had to get on with his plan. He had to make certain that Amy would come down to the cellar soon and see her lost Little Lydia!

Suppose this carton was thought to be just summer toys and books of Amy's? Leave it down here all winter, until off again the family would go to Truro? Well, he must not let that happen! Little Lydia was not a cellar doll, a tiny banger on pipes, a tiny plumber. She belonged upstairs with Amy and her family, with her friend, Clarissa, and with Wags, with Bear and all her other dolls, Lydia, Big, who had swallowed a thermometer...all the friends and family listed in Amy's *Who's Who Book.*

He zoomied open the dusty cellar window above Amy's carton, then he sped across the street to the top of a lamppost, where he had a fine view of number 3017!

Amy and Clarissa were standing at the open bay window of the big second-floor bedroom where they always played, drew pictures, wrote stories or made them up, or listened to records. The curtains were parted and the window flung open as far as possible. Amy and Clarissa were stretching out their arms as though to bring in all the beauty of the washed-clean outside world. They opened their mouths wide to gulp down some of this beauty.

"Why, Clarissa!" exclaimed Amy. "There's a rainbow! Suppose we had the zoomie-zoomies and could fly through it!"

On the floor beneath them, the first floor, Papa and Mama were standing in the bay window of the parlor, looking up and down the street, getting used to being home. Some branches had broken off, but none from their old gingko tree with its strong-smelling orange fruit, rolling about like Ping-Pong balls in the last slight breeze of the storm.

Wags was standing close to Papa, front paws on the windowsill. He was sniffing the air and looking happy and ridiculous with Papa's old sock dangling lopsided from the side of his mouth. Once in a while he went to the door leading to the cellar, scratched at it, said "Woof!" and came back.

Jimmy McGee, from the top of his lamppost, took all this in. Now for his plan!

He took his strong little thunder and lightning bolt box out of his stovepipe hat. He put it to his ear and listened. Good! There were still faint rumblings of thunder, and he felt tingly little lightning vibrations along with the thunder. He was happy that neither of his prized little thunder and lightning bolts had worn out all their strength while handing it out, by means of the bolt box, right and left to the refugees in the winter headquarters.

This tiny little streak of lightning, not even as large as a lightning bug, could not now possibly hurt anybody, not even an ant. But he hoped the rumbly little thunderbolt was still loud enough for people in Number 3017 to hear it and wonder what it was.

All of them then would race for the cellar to look and to listen. Then Amy, of course, would spot her little long-lost do-nothing doll, Little Lydia!

He took careful aim at the cellar window he had left ajar. Then he opened up his thunder and lightning bolt box, and out shot his tiny zigzag tail of lightning and along with it the comfortable rumbling of his thunderbolt, somewhat louder than even Jimmy McGee, the expert, had expected. Its comfortable rumbly-jumbly rolling sound could be heard not only in the cellar of Amy's house, but all up and down Garden Lane!

Cardinal Bird, refugee, singing "Tweet tweet-tweet," flew to the tiptop of Jimmy McGee's lamppost and settled there. Along with Jimmy McGee, he waited.

Jimmy McGee grinned. He waited for the people. They came.

"O-o-oh!" said Amy. "Did you see that lightning?"

"And hear that thunder!" said Clarissa, putting her hands over her ears in case there might be more and really loud claps!

They ran downstairs.

Papa was saying, "Have we been struck by

lightning?" He had opened the cellar door but was guarding it like a dragon with his outstretched arms. He wanted to go down first, make sure of...what?

"Couldn't have been thunder and lightning," Mama said. "But it did seem to have come from our cellar. Look at the sky, though, not a cloud in it! All clear blue...pure!"

"Maybe a pipe burst!" said Papa. "Let's go down. Whatever it was, it's gone away."

So everyone, including Wags, who beat them all down, practically sliding there on his belly, raced to the cellar.

"Nothing's wrong down here," said Mama. "Maybe we imagined it!"

"Imagined...pooh!" said Amy. "It *was* thunder and lightning, wasn't it, Clarissa?"

"Why yes, of course," said Clarissa. She covered her ears again as she always did at the mere mention of thunder. With no bed to crawl under, she stuck close to Amy's mother.

"Well, I just plain don't see how it could have been," said Papa. "With such a clearing of the air...no rain, no wind, no trees blowing..."

"Anyway," said Mama. "If it had been thunder and lightning, Wags would have hidden behind the dining room door or gone into a closet and howled."

"Well," said Papa. "No pipes have burst. All of us, so tired from such a long drive all in one day, skirting the edge of Hurricane Lobelia, wondering if we'd run into its path...but hey! Look at that window swinging there, half open, half closed...

"I don't remember opening it. Why would I open that particular window? It would not have been easy...all windows being stuck from being tightly closed all summer. Why that one? Beats me!"

"Maybe the wind blew it open. There *was* a storm, you know," said Mama. "Well, there *was* a noise down here. It *did* sound like thunder. Four people and a dog don't imagine the same thing at the same time. But come on up. Let's get something to eat."

But Amy said, "I'm going to take some of my toys from my carton upstairs to my room."

"Well, you and Clarissa can do that," said Papa. "My back aches!"

Mama rubbed his back. "It was a long, hard drive. Let's go up. You rest on the divan while I fix a bite or two."

But Wags stayed behind. He sniffed in all the corners of the cellar with Papa's sock dangling from his mouth, and he came over to Amy's carton. He had cobwebs in his nose and had to sneeze! In order to do this, he had to drop Papa's sock. Since he happened to be standing over Amy's carton, which she and Clarissa were about to unload, Papa's sock fell on top of the toys!

"Oh, Wags!" scolded Amy. "That dirty, wet sandy sock is on my nice toys."

She picked it up, and he eagerly grabbed it. It was almost as though it were part of him. And by the dim light of a dusty electric light bulb swinging over her toy box, Amy gasped in astonishment at what she saw. At first she was struck dumb!

Then she said, "Clarissa! Clarissa! Look!"

Clarissa knelt down and looked. "Why..." she said. "Not...not..."

"Yes!" said Amy. "Little Lydia! My Little Lydia! She's here. Right here on top of my *Who's Who Book*! Remember I tucked my book in at the last moment this morning along with Little Lydia's blue shawl? And, look! Little Lydia is lying on her real, right L page!"

"I know, I see," said Clarissa.

"And," Amy went on, "she was not there when Papa packed the car, not there when we left Truro, not there when Papa dragged this carton down the cellar when we got home. My book wasn't even open then. I don't think it was..."

"How'd Little Lydia get here then?" demanded Clarissa. "We haven't seen her since she was grabbed by that huge wave, Monstrous!"

Amy thought for a moment. Gently she picked Little Lydia up and studied her. Then she said in solemn tones, "Clarissa! You know what? Little Lydia must have come in the window with that strange little thunder and lightning bolt..."

"Of course," said Clarissa in delight. "With the thunder and the lightning...through the window there, a little ajar..."

Amy wrapped Little Lydia in her blue shawl, put her in her pocket with her *Who's Who Book.* "Let's take this whole carton upstairs. I don't like its being down here. Another thunder and lightning bolt might make off with something else, or even try to recapture Little Lydia!"

They were about to do this, but Wags kept sniffing around and around the carton. "He smells the sock he dropped in there," said Amy. "But, Wags, you have Papa's sock back now. It's not in the box anymore, is it? You know it's dangling from your mouth."

"Woof!" Wags circled around the box again and again.

"Oh-h! You know what?" said Amy. "He saw Mama run back to the cottage to get his spare sock and drop it in the back somewhere...here! And he wants that sock, even if it is clean. When we empty the box, we'll find the other sock. But come on. Yo-ho-ho, up the stairs we go!"

They dragged the carton up the cellar stairs to the kitchen, through the dining room, around the bend, through the hall, and then, gasping, up the stairs—none too easy because Wags went along with them sniffing at it all the way from one side or the other, squeezing himself between it and the wall to make sure what he smelled was still there!

But they made it anyway to the second floor, and they put the carton on the blue velvet-covered cushion on the window seat in the bay window.

"Phew!" said Amy. "Hot!" She took Little Lydia out of her pocket. "Clarissa," she said. "Don't you think it's interesting that Little Lydia was on top of the page that has her name on it in my *Who's Who Book*?"

Wags kept bothering them, trying to look in the carton. Amy handed him his spare sock. "There now, Wags. Take this down to Mama... maybe she'll wash one or the other."

Wags was suspicious of this sock, but it seemed to smell O.K. to him, so he left to carry his two trophies to Mama. It was a hard trip down the stairs, but he slid most of the way on his belly.

"Maybe," said Clarissa, "Little Lydia *was* in that other sock, been hanging on the line at The Bizzy Bee a long time."

"Oh, no," said Amy. "I don't think so. Anyway, there's a hole in the toe of that one."

So Amy and Clarissa returned to pondering the strangeness of the return of Little Lydia. "And she's been missing for such a long time!" said Clarissa.

"Look at that page in my book," said Amy. "You see those smudges? There're smudges by 'Lydia, Little,' and there're smudges by 'McGee,

Jimmy'...new smudges, not the old ones that we've already seen."

"Oh, yes," said Clarissa. "'McGee, Jimmy... little fellow...plumber...banger on pipes,'" recited Clarissa.

"And, don't forget *hero*!" said Amy. "Smudges! Maybe Jimmy McGee made those smudges. Maybe he's the one who found Little Lydia...brought her back here in thunder, lightning, and in 'ren'! 'Ren' is the way Mama always says 'rain.'

"And that's what she always says when there's a bad storm...and Little Lydia did come back in thunder, lightning, and in 'ren'!"

"And there was a 'ren-bow,'" said Clarissa.

"Yes," said Amy. "Gone away now, beautiful sky now! And we can say 'Hurrah' for Jimmy McGee. He truly is a *hero*!"

Amy thought a minute. The window was wide open. "Clarissa," she said, "if Jimmy McGee did get Little Lydia back to me, should we shout out into the air a thank-you to Jimmy McGee? He might hear."

They did this. In unison Amy and Clarissa shouted, "Thank you, Jimmy McGee. You are a *hero*!"

There was no answer, but Jimmy McGee had heard and was pleased.

"It's clear out," said Clarissa. "Soon the stars will shine."

Amy was still studying Little Lydia. "Clarissa!" she said. "Feel Little Lydia. Does she tingle?"

Clarissa held Little Lydia close to her ear. "Why, yes," she said. "She does tingle a little, I think."

"Proves it," said Amy. "Been on lightning. Probably's had lots of adventures since I lost her in the ocean," said Amy. "Maybe she's even had the zoomie-zoomies."

"It must have been a very curious adventure for a do-nothing doll," said Clarissa. "Or for any kind of doll."

Amy picked up her clown doll, sitting with the rest of her dolls on the small divan. "Hello, Zazoom," she said. "Did you miss me? I tell you what, Clarissa. Let's put Zazoom on the windowsill, lean him against the frame, so he can get a breath of fresh air, too."

"Oh, yes," said Clarissa, "where he can look out across the street."

Amy fluffed up his rumpled red clown suit and shook his tousled yellow yarn hair, hugged him, and laughed. Then she deposited him safely on the windowsill, where, if he could see, he would have a fine view of the lamppost across the street. "There," she said. "Don't fall."

Then she closed her *Who's Who Book* and put it in a niche in the little roll-top desk her grandpa had made for her, exactly like his big one. With Little Lydia clutched in her hand, she and Clarissa then went outside and sat down, Clarissa on the top step of the stoop and Amy in the little rope swing that hung from the fragile young pine tree to the left of the steps. Amy swung gently, happily. She held Little Lydia in her right hand and let her pretend she was holding the rope, too.

Mama came to the door and said, "Aren't you hungry? I've brought you a plate of little sandwiches and some milk. Have a little picnic here!"

Sitting there then, watching the stars come out, Amy and Clarissa ate their suppers.

"Oh! How pretty it is here!" said Amy.

"Yes," said Clarissa.

Across the street, from the top of the lamppost Cardinal Bird was singing his good-night song. Then suddenly he flew away, a flash of bright red against the darkening sky. He was heading for Mount Rose Park.

From his place at the top of the lamppost across the street, Jimmy McGee looked over at Number 3017 where Amy and Clarissa were having their snack on the front stoop. Little Lydia was on Amy's plate, joining in. This was a real homecoming party for her! Jimmy McGee smiled. It all looked pretty to him.

He thought about the events of the summer. Finally, everything had gone the way he had hoped it would. He had always wanted to catch thunder and lightning bolts, teeny, tiny ones, to round out his bolt collection, and he had. And he had used them well; he had let them loose on a special occasion, which today had certainly been.

First there had been the carnival of refugees in his headquarters. But, best of all was the rescue and the return of Little Lydia, lost for so long, but now home again at last with Amy. He had never had it in mind to rescue any little lost anything, but he *had* rescued her twice...once from the great wave, Monstrous, and finally from the electrical effect of the bolt charges. And there she was now, having supper with

Amy, author of the *Who's Who Book*! Hero! That's what Amy said about him in that book, and it had bothered him all summer.

He thought, "Well, if that's the way you get to be a *hero,* it had been fun."

Just to test the word, he bebopped, "Fun!"

There was no reply from Little Lydia, sitting on Amy's supper plate at Number 3017.

Right after Cardinal Bird flew off, Jimmy McGee made his own rounds; and when he finished these, he zoomie-zoomied to his winter headquarters, where he had to do some straightening up after the grand jamboree.

It seemed to him that his headquarters echoed still from the songs and sounds and speeches of the refugees. So in zoomie-zoomie time, he created an operetta. The name was *Refugees from Hurricane Lobelia.* He set it to music and outlined the solos, the duets, the dance sequences. When finished, he put it in one of his music scrolls.

In the distance, coming from over at the tool shed in Dunbarton Oaks Park, he could hear the voices of the refugees. It was almost as though they were having a rehearsal of his operetta. Anyway, it was fun to hear...the basso solo of Froggy, Ms. Red Hen a full orchestra in herself, and of course, the soprano voice of Cardinal Bird, whose duet with Filibuster, the tenor, was the most applauded.

And then off he went on his nighttime rounds. Lights in 3017 Garden Lane were off, except for a dim one in the hall outside Amy's room, so he zoomie-zoomied away.

In bed Clarissa said, "Amy?"

"M-m-m?" said Amy.

"What about Jimmy McGee?"

"Well, Clarissa. He's off on his rounds. But you know what? I made up a song about him . . . it just came to me. It goes like this:

Oh, Jimmy McGee, a plumber is he.
He bangs on the pipes to wake you and me.
And he bangs on the gong in the
    schoolyard, you hear?
So you won't be marked late, not once the
    whole year!

"Like it?" asked Amy.

"Oh yes," said Clarissa. "I'll learn it."

"Remember, don't you, that school begins the day after tomorrow?" said Amy.

"Yes . . . oh, yes," said Clarissa.

"And, Clarissa," said Amy. "Remember your alphabet."

"Yes," said Clarissa. "If I forget anything, I just have to think of your *Who's Who Book*! A...Amy, B...Bear, C...Clarissa..."

"You don't need to go through the whole book, Clarissa. It's late. Just tell me the ending."

"Z...zoomie-zoomies: a magic that can make people who have it do curious things."

"M-m-m," said Clarissa.

They both said "magic" together and made a wish. "May your wish and my wish come true," they said.

ELEANOR ESTES (1906–1988) grew up in West Haven, Connecticut, which she renamed Cranbury for her classic stories about the Moffat and Pye families. A children's librarian for many years, she launched her writing career with the publication of *The Moffats* in 1941. Two of her outstanding books about the Moffats—*Rufus M.* and *The Middle Moffat*—were awarded Newbery Honors, as was her short novel *The Hundred Dresses.* She won the Newbery Medal for *Ginger Pye* in 1952.